Steve works as a dispensing optician and is currently living in Somerset with his wife, two sons, daughter and two rather large Leonberger dogs. He spends his relaxing time (when not being hounded by the dogs) trying to play guitar and writing songs and has been designing and developing a board game on and off for the past ten years!

To Donna

All the best

You suddenly appeared and I pulled you close, such a blubbering wreck as I kissed your nose, and later that day I wrote a letter to you, the contents of which I now haven't a clue, but soon you will read for the year is near, my emotional writings to you my dear
Ellie,
Colourful lots xxx

To Lewey Lee, Squeezebox and Gibbs,
Just file this next to my CD, or you could even read it.

To Avril,
True, it's not your cup of coffee, but give it a stir sometime, you never know…xx

Steve Bennett

A MINDFUL AFFLATUS

AUSTIN MACAULEY PUBLISHERS™

LONDON • CAMBRIDGE • NEW YORK • SHARJAH

A CIP catalogue record for this title is available from the British Library.

Based on true events. The names of individuals have been changed to maintain anonymity.

ISBN 9781788235358 (Paperback)
ISBN 9781528956581 (ePub e-book)

www.austinmacauley.com

First Published (2019)
Austin Macauley Publishers Ltd
25 Canada Square
Canary Wharf
London
E14 5LQ

There were two members of my family who unconditionally supported me during the writing of this book. Their complete attentiveness and devotion never wavered, and I would like to say how grateful I was for their efforts to keep me warm in the conservatory during the long winter evenings.

Lying across my feet really did work!

Max and Teddy, thank you.

Based on a True Event

"I've never seen such a bloody clean bike!"

His words were laden with sarcasm as he sat astride his mud-splattered machine, like a general about to go into battle.

My bike was better than clean, it was immaculate; I was always polishing it. But in this situation, I suddenly didn't want it to be shiny any more. I wanted it to be dirty and streetwise like theirs.

His two 'soldiers' laughed and swore in approval of his ridiculing observation and excitedly over-revved their 250s, in an attempt to create acclamation sounds from their engines.

I felt uncomfortable. I didn't know where this was going.

They had approached us and instigated the dialogue, taking great pride in telling us that they were uninsured, untaxed and seemingly unbothered about anything.

We just listened and cautiously laughed at the right times, having an almost envious appreciation of these bad lads of the night...

Suddenly, his bald rear tyre revolved into life, spitting out dirt and dust in one fast short spurt of antisocial defiance.

"Let's race to Harlow!" he yelled.

It was a statement rather than a command, but we reacted. He wanted us to join them.

I looked at Mike.

He was already manoeuvring his Suzuki, and there was excitement in his eyes as he glanced at me.

We didn't know these lads; in fact, we were about to call it a night before they appeared on the scene, but here we were; about to go into highway battle with the nightriders...

We took off up the A11, like bats out of hell, with the bad lads shouting and screaming, like banshees, as they weaved their bikes from side to side in front of us, in a display of complete disregard to road use normality. We watched in disbelief as they cut through the intersection to ride the wrong way up the opposite side of the dual carriageway, then crossing back over at the next break to reappear in front of us again, to continue with their crazy show.

They were mad, absolutely irrational, and we were being sucked into this fanatical early-morning charge by the exhilaration and anticipation, that was increasing at every second.

Wow…! What a rush.

We soon hit a long straight piece of road, and I lowered myself down onto the tank. I was barely peeking over the top of the rev counter in a vain streamlining attempt to keep up with them all as two-stroke smoke peppered the warm night air in front of me.

Come on! Come on! Faster! Faster!

My normal world of law-abiding regulations, full of consequential thoughts and concerns, had vanished. I was now living completely for the moment. All that was significant lay directly ahead of me in a one-way blinkered tunnel of sight and sound.

I wanted to go faster; I needed to go faster…

…and then suddenly…he appeared!

WHERE did he come from?

My soaring feelings of adrenaline-pumping excitement immediately plateaued and dramatically fell into one of trepidation and panic as I saw that he was driving level with me on the other side of the road.

His outstretched motionless hand was a signal to stop; in fact, it was more; it was telling me to go back. It was a strange feeling, but I knew that's what he wanted me to do. They were immediate thoughts, and I just knew.

I couldn't see him clearly, but he was there behind the wheel: a dark figure of authority, with a statuesque extended arm aimed towards me. It seemed to project an invisible line that I should not pass…a line that he did not want me to pass.

I kept looking into the car.

Had we almost stopped moving?

It felt like we had. Time seemed to have slowed right down. I was somehow connected with the car…I couldn't change focus,

I couldn't look away. I must look away...I must look at the road...

"Go back! Go back!"

I slammed on the brakes and watched his car slingshot ahead of me.

Did I hear him say that? It was a shout more than anything, and it certainly snapped me out of the hypnotic hold the car had on me. *How could I have heard him?* The passenger window wasn't down! Blimey, that was really weird, and I say I was connected with the car, I think it was with him...I felt the connection was with him somehow...

I watched as he sped after the others. He wasn't slowing...he didn't want me; he wanted to catch the bigger, faster fish. I felt really odd as my mind subconsciously was analysing what had just happened, and how it happened. I couldn't have heard him. I just simply couldn't have!

I had come to a halt now, and there was just the sound of my bike engine ticking over as I viewed everyone disappearing around the bend in the far distance.

Was it an unmarked police car? Well, that's what I had assumed, and I felt relieved that I hadn't been officially stopped. I stared ahead down the empty road, almost expecting them to reappear and come charging back towards me. No, that wasn't going to happen, but something would, I had a strange feeling that something definitely would!

I turned around and rode slowly back home.

My head was buzzing with what had transpired over the last ten minutes or so. I felt I was jumping from one emotion to another. And now I was concerned...concerned about what was going to happen to Mike.

I cut my engine when I saw the lay-by and glided quietly to a stop. We always met and chatted here for a while after a ride before going back to our respective homes; and tonight, I'm sure, would be no exception.

I sat and waited. After ten minutes or so, I started to listen more definitely for the distinctive sounds of his 250. He'd be along soon after his 'talk' with the police. I'd hung my crash helmet over the right mirror, had folded my arms, and was impatiently listening into the calm early-morning air.

Come on, Mike.

I was feeling more and more agitated and unsettled. *Should I ride back?* There was only one answer to that, and I had already agreed with it.

I started the engine, put my helmet back on and rode towards the A11 and then onwards towards Harlow.

The only racing going on now was in my mind. Perhaps they'd all been arrested. Perhaps the nightrider gang were REALLY bad lads, and the police were now obviously assuming that Mike was one of them too!

I swung right at the second roundabout and headed towards the town centre. The roads were so quiet and deserted. Wouldn't it be superb if they were like this all the time?

That thought soon evaporated as I quickly focused on something going on further up the road. I could see a figure sitting on the kerb edge, looking towards me, which I soon realised was Mike. I then noticed loads of what seemed to be sheets of paper strewn everywhere as I tried to digest the scene that lay before me. Oh no, hold on…I've seen this before. I've dreamt this, I know I have…

There was a bike lying in the road and another that was parked on its side stand, which I recognised as being Mike's Suzuki.

He raised a hand in a dejected greeting as I pulled over. I glanced back down at the paper in the road again. The 'memory' was so clear now. The paper was everywhere, and it was reflecting in the lights from the yellow street lamps. I could see that there was also bits of plastic and metal intermingled, and I soon realised that they were bike parts.

I walked over to Mike with my hands out in front of me…

"You're not going to believe this, but this was in one of my dreams, it was just like this…paper all over the road!"

"That's our cancer and polio leaflets. My top box burst open when I came off…and thanks a bloody million for not warning me!"

(We did a money collection every two weeks going to certain houses, and some were a bit off the beaten track, so we used it as a good excuse to ride out.

The front part of the leaflet was always made glossy, and that was the bright reflection that I could see.)

"And where d'you go?" he continued. "One minute you were there, the next you'd gone…"

Mike's tone of voice was one of annoyance. I did feel guilty for leaving him, and I definitely shouldn't have started talking with the dream. I knew that he was aware of some of the 'premonitions' that I'd been having over the past few years. But there was no way I could have prevented this. It only just came to me when I saw the paper everywhere anyway.

"I know, I'm sorry…the police car freaked me out. So what happened? Where are the others? Has he gone after them?"

As I was speaking, both our attentions were being drawn across the road to a car that had just pulled up, and the driver's window was being wound down.

"Is he OK?"

"Yeah, we're fine, no worries…thanks a lot," I replied in an overzealous reassuring manner as Mike stood up on cue.

I knew Mike was alright; I just needed to get us away from here and back home.

"Do you want me to do anything? Do you need an ambulance?" said the rather nervous lady driver.

"No thanks, no honest, we're fine."

I could tell that she had only morally stopped rather than for any genuine concern. She understandably just wanted to get on her way, and her car was moving forward slightly in gear as she spoke. She soon drove off, edging slightly to one side to avoid the motorbike that lay in the road.

I immediately went over and pulled it back up. Blimey, it was in a right old state. The front wheel was completely bent in, the forks were pushed under the tank, the rev counter/speedo mounting was non-existent…it really was in one heck of a mess!

The wheels were jammed, so I slowly struggled dragging it a bit closer to the kerb and then let it fall back on its side, sort of half on, half off the road. It weighed a ton. I looked over at Mike. He'd sat back down again.

"Are you OK?"

"Yeah, I'm alright…come on, let's get out of here," he said seriously as he stood back up again and walked over to his machine.

"Where's the bloke?" I said, pointing at the wrecked bike.

"He went off with the others…"

"What?" I said, with a completely puzzled look on my face.

"I know, don't worry about it...I'll tell you later," came the pressing response.

He pulled his helmet back on and started his bike.

"What shall we do about this?" I said, pointing to all the paper and debris that littered the road.

"Leave it! Come on...I just wanna get back."

I restarted my Honda; and at a sedate pace, we made our way out of Harlow and back down the A11. Mike was alright, just a bit shocked I guess, and his bike seemed alright too, thank goodness; although I could see him looking down at the tank every now and then as if checking something.

We were soon approaching 'our lay-by', and I wasn't sure whether he would pull in or not, but he did. We turned off our engines, took off our helmets, and it was there that he then began to tell me what had actually happened.

The three nightriders were racing side by side in front of him when one of them seemed to suddenly go straight over the handlebars, like he'd hit a brick wall. Mike had braked hard to avoid collision and had skidded out of control and had toppled over.

The crashed nightrider was in a bit of a bad way, and there was a mad panic to get him up off the road and get him away from the scene.

He managed to get on the back of one of the bikes, and they rode off towards the town centre.

"So, what about the copper? Wasn't he trying to stop them?" I said.

It was at this point that we entered the twilight zone when Mike voiced that he had no idea of what I was going on about.

I elaborated further; in fact, I went on and on about it. But, he absolutely insisted that...

"There was never a car chasing us!"

Prologue

In 1982, I moved away from the family home to take on the role of a managing dispensing optician at an optical practice in South London. I had recently qualified in the profession and was quite nervous at the step-up and unfamiliarity of my new post. But at the same time, I was very excited of being able to live away from home and was really looking forward to experiencing my first true taste of independence at the ripe old age of 23.

My new living abode was an oldie worldie flat, with high ceilings, beams and pillars, that was situated on the second floor (which was the top floor), above the actual opticians practice.

On the first floor, directly below my flat, lived a lady of 40 odd years called Jackie. She was about 5'2" tall and of medium ladies' build, who would always be seen in bright-coloured baggy cardigans and dark, below the knee-length skirts. She invariably seemed to wear dark-coloured tights too, with little black pixie boots, when going out. She was a lovely woman, who never seemed to let anything worry her, almost to the point though where I would often doubt her awareness of the importance of the particular situation that she was in at the time. Still, nothing was ever too much trouble for her, but I'm sure many people took advantage of her incredibly nice and easy-going placid nature.

Her flat had no real furniture to mention, with a television set and a record player being the only highlights of the living room, and she seemed to live on food that was mostly obtained from the health food store where she worked. She would frequently mother me with her incredibly tasty baked potatoes which always seemed to have a rather interesting smell about them, and she unfailingly seemed to have one wrapped in baking foil, warming in the oven, ready to offer. Mmm, and I always felt rather good after I'd eaten one too...which I'm sure was no coincidence!

Our flats were accessed by a door from the street, which would take us along an indoor corridor that ran along the side of the practice, up an enclosed concrete staircase at the back, which led out onto an open flat roof, then up a few more steps and into a short covered walkway; that was 'our hallway.'

On opening the front door to my flat, I would climb a steep, fairly wide wooden staircase, which turned at 90 degrees to the right halfway up, then 90 degrees right again, which allowed me to walk directly onto the living/dining room floor. First left was my bedroom and second left was another long corridor, which led down to the kitchen, with a bathroom halfway down on the right. The corridor dipped amazingly in the middle, giving the impression that you were walking down a slight slope and back up the other side, and boy did it creak. I always felt that one day it would suddenly collapse and I'd end up in Jackie's flat below!

The flat was furnished with a 1970s orange-coloured sofa and armchair, which both had superb, wide, black-coloured, sloping vinyl arm rests. There was also a rather large, chunky, heavy dining table (I could hardly lift the thing), an assortment of old wooden dining chairs, and a rather tall double bed. I certainly understood the expression 'climbing into bed' all too well!

The optical practice had two part-time receptionists, who were Eileen and Carla, three ophthalmic medical practitioners (known as doctors), who worked on various full and half days to perform the eye testing; and finally a dispensing optician who sorted out the spectacle lenses and the frames side of it all and who hopefully was managing it all correctly...and that was me!

It was a lovely family-type working atmosphere, and I got to know Eileen and Carla very well over the four to five years that I worked there.

In the early days, I always felt that I was trying to establish myself with the local traders. I was given the 'new boy on the block' routine from all of them. It was comparable to a stranger walking into a village pub for the first time; although, in my case, it seemed to go on for much longer. I felt very awkward sometimes and very frustrated too; but gradually, I realised that I was becoming accepted, and I soon began getting invitations to traders 'get-together' type functions. I must be honest, I found those events rather boring and all a bit of an act, but it was very pleasing in my mind to know that I was finally being received as a member of the local trading community.

True friends came much quicker and easier, thank goodness, and I must admit many came by the way of Jackie. She was always hosting parties in her flat; and more often or not, I ended up in there too, sitting on the floor, talking and drinking with them all… and it was at one of these social gatherings where I met Johnny and Chris.

Now Johnny was around 30 years old I'd say, of stocky build, with a lightly tanned chiselled face. He was about 5'8'' in height, with pushed-back thin black hair that fought hard to cover the head that was gradually being exposed beneath. He came across as the 'Godfather' of the group, but he never advertised the reality…it just seemed to be quietly accepted within the circle of friends. If something wasn't right, something needed 'sorting out', 'go and have a word with Johnny', I heard that said many times. He definitely had a sort of an air about him, and I often noticed men in the street discreetly acknowledging his presence with a nod of the head as they walked by!

Now, Chris, I reckon, was a little younger than John; much slimmer and a little taller too, with thick brown hair. He always gave me the impression that he was trying to emulate John, but he did it in a non-condescending way that was full of genuine warmth and concern for everyone too, and you couldn't help but like him for it.

I never felt awkward with either of them, and they both became good friends. We would often meet up in a particular pub for a drink, and then walk down the road to my flat for a nightcap, and it was at one of these evenings in June 1986 when it all started…although I far from realised it at the time!

Friday, June 13th
A Plan Is Hatched

I met them both around 8:00 p.m., and we drank and talked and drank some more until closing time, after which we made our customary journey back down the road to my flat, which was about a five-minute walk away. We were all quite light-headed and merry but definitely not drunk.

As soon as we got in, I put some music on and then went down to the kitchen to get some drinks from the fridge, whilst Johnny spread himself out on the sofa and Chris slumped down in the armchair.

Now, almost right above the stairs in the ceiling was a very large attic hatch. It must have been about 4 feet square, it was huge, and I'd often said that one day I'd like to try and get up there to find out what was on the other side. But it was positioned in such an awkward place, that to even reach the hatch, I'd either require the use of a long ladder, or I'd need to be innovative and build some kind of platform.

Well…we didn't have the long ladder, but we did have a load of dining chairs and a couple of old rickety wooden stools, which tonight together were going to be our very creative and improvised scaffolding!

I cannot remember who instigated it, but before long, we were 'merrily' putting it all together. Thoughts of falling off and tumbling down the stairs didn't even enter my head; as after about ten minutes or so of rather entertaining construction, it was more or less completed, and I started the climb to the top. As I ascended, I looked up, and immediately I could tell I was barely going to reach the ceiling. John reckoned that if I could get the hatch open, I would just about be able to poke my head through.

I got to the top and held on to the recessed hatch edges for support. I was standing slightly bent, with the side of my head

18

and the palms of my hands against the hatch door, as I began to give it a steady push upwards, straightening my body at the same time. It made a cracking sound at first as it broke free from where it had probably sat untouched for years…and boy was it heavy, but I pushed it up and managed to manipulate it over to one side.

So picture this…there I was, standing perilously upright, holding on to the hatch edge, with my head JUST poking through into the attic itself…(Johnny was right).

"What can you see, what can you see?" they both said, almost in excited urgent unison, which sounded quite funny coming from them, as I stretched my neck to better my view.

All I could see was a slight reflection from something that was further back in the attic that I immediately thought was a mirror, but that was all I could actually focus upon…I couldn't see anything else…

And then…

Woooooooooooooosh!

An incredibly strong force of cold air shot down my entire body.

It startled me with its suddenness, its strength, and how cold and direct it was…so much so that I reacted by gripping the hatch sides even tighter.

It surprised us all for a moment, with a three way expletive response, but it was over in an instant, and we disregarded it almost immediately with laughter and jocular comments; although in my mind, it did make me feel a little odd, as it felt like the air had squeezed my body when it passed down. Anyway, the thought was there but merely a fleeting one; and the attic exploration soon came to an end too. I couldn't really see anything up there as it was so dark; and annoyingly, I didn't have a torch, and I most certainly couldn't climb any higher…so I repositioned the hatch door and gingerly made my way down.

We didn't really expand afterwards on what had happened either. It was simply cold air being let out of an attic that hadn't been opened for donkey's years; and of course at the time, there really wasn't anything else to connect with it…so what was there to discuss?

In Chris's words, it was discarded as a 'bloody waste of time.'

It was probably the effects of the drink that had dulled any instant investigation into what had actually just transpired anyway.

It happened…we swore…we laughed…and that was that!

Saturday, June 14th
Hits of the '80s

I was working in the practice up until 12:30 p.m., as we always closed for the afternoon on a Saturday. I came downstairs as usual at about 8:40 a.m. and prepared the place for the morning 'rush'. Carla was working with me today, and she came in around 8:50 a.m., and I had her coffee waiting for her on the desk out in the back office. She was a pretty lady in her early 40s, quite cheeky in her ways, with a mischievous smile that always made me think that she was thinking a lot more than she let on. She habitually wore close-fitting, bright-coloured revealing dresses, and always had bare legs, even in the winter. She was very hard-working and always meticulously ensured that she had completed everything that needed to be done before she left to go home.

When Carla was with me on a Saturday, she would always want to hear my agenda for the weekend. So as we sat down in the back office, I enlightened her of my plans of being a DJ at a friend's wedding reception, which was taking place near my parents' home up in Hertfordshire later that night. I had a double deck record turntable disco unit and two 50 watt speakers that I used as my own home hi-fi; and on the odd occasion, I would offer my services as a DJ for a bit of fun. I must be honest though…I enjoyed doing it, but I was always worried that I could potentially ruin that persons 'big night' if the deck ever broke down as I never had a back-up or anything like that.

Still, it never stopped me, and the fun of doing it always outweighed the worry…just!

The morning shot by as it always did on a Saturday; and after we had cleared up, it must have been around 1:00 p.m. when I said goodbye to Carla and went upstairs to make myself a sandwich for lunch. I had left a few records out by the disco unit as I'd been thinking about a few new mixes that I wanted to trial in the afternoon before I left.

So there I am, standing in front of the deck.

I must've been mixing and playing music for about 30 minutes or so, and I was thinking that I'd better start getting a move on as I wanted to spend some time at my parents' house before going on to the reception.

It was a lovely warm June afternoon. I was wearing a dark blue flower-patterned capped t-shirt and a pair of red baggy trousers (very DJ!) that I'd bought from a clothing store called 'Flip' in Covent Garden.

I had the headphones in my left hand, with the left cup held against my ear, listening to the music as my right hand adjusted the controls on the deck…

SMACK!

I felt a sharp and fast slap on the top of my bare right arm, and I immediately ripped the headphone from my ear and recoiled back in alarm!

(I've got goose pimples now as I'm telling you this even after all this time.)

I span around to look behind me…

Someone had just hit me! Someone had just hit me on the arm!

I looked around the room…there was no one to be seen…I was on my own.

…I quickly bent forward and stopped the music playing and looked around the room again.

I then looked at the top of my arm and rubbed it. I could feel it slightly tingling.

I started to move my arm up and down as if I was doing a one-winged chicken impression.

Did I catch it on something? I was trying to make it happen again.

One of the old wooden pillars in the flat was close to me…but not that close. There was no way I could have caught it on that.

I looked at my arm again…oh blimey! It was beginning to redden where it had been 'hit'!

What! This was crazy!

I stood there moving my arm around once more. I was wearing a capped t-shirt, so there were no shirt cuffs or anything hanging loose that could have done it; and the headphone I was holding was in my left hand, so there was no way the dangling cord could have caught my right arm.

I kept looking around the room.

I just couldn't make out what had happened…I really couldn't.

I walked down into the kitchen and made myself an orange squash, then came back into the living room and stood staring at the deck as I made light work of the drink.

I felt the top of my arm again. I was truly perplexed…

Right! Come on…forget it…focus on matters in hand…I've got to get organised and get going…

It was on my mind as I loaded the car that afternoon. The red mark did seem to fade rather quickly, but it had been red…well, pink anyway. Something had caught the top of my arm, and I couldn't give a rational explanation. But by the time I had hit the road, new thoughts were dominating my mind as the nerves and excitement of the evening ahead had completely suppressed anything else.

Sunday, June 15th
Late-Night Dessert

I stayed over at my parents' house that night after the wedding reception, and I returned to the flat quite late on Sunday evening.

I stopped the car outside the front of the practice and unloaded my music gear, leaving it all just inside the door in the corridor. Then, I drove my car around to the residential parking area that I used near the church and walked back. I opened the side door and pushed in the light plunger switch on the wall to light up the length of the corridor. It was one of those timed light systems, though the set time was NEVER long enough to allow you to actually walk down the corridor and up the stairs to the flats while it remained on! It always seemed to 'de-plunge' you into darkness well before.

I picked up one of the speakers by its handle and walked fast down the corridor, making my way up to the flat as quickly as I could. Sure enough, the light went off halfway up the first flight of stairs, just before I reached the second plunger light switch…useless thing.

I arrived at my front door, unlocked and opened it, and then switched on the stair light. I then began lugging the speaker up the final lot of stairs.

When I reached the top, I put the speaker down, stood still and looked into the living room. Something had caught my eye that was glinting in the light from the stairs. It was lying on the carpet in the middle of the room, and I recognised it immediately as a spoon from the kitchen. It was my silver dessert spoon which had a thick, black, long plastic handle. It was the only dessert spoon I had.

I turned on the main living room light and went over and picked it up. Now that was strange, because believe it or not, I'm quite a tidy chap, and I would always make sure that the flat was

24

fairly clean and uncluttered when I left it in the morning to go down to work, OR as in this case if I had gone away for the weekend.

I picked up the spoon and put it on the table and then ran downstairs to fetch the rest of my gear.

It was soon dismissed in my mind as just something that I had overlooked. It was only a spoon for goodness' sake, and I suppose I could have quite easily have dropped it there before I left yesterday afternoon.

It was odd though that it was right in the middle of the room. Surely, I would've seen it as I walked out of the flat, wouldn't I...?

Monday, June 16th
Sofa Not So Good

I got up at the last possible moment, giving me just enough time to have breakfast and get ready to go downstairs to work.

Living above your place of work certainly has its advantages, with regular sleep-ins and no traffic problems to worry about. But it does have its disadvantages too, as the expression 'taking your work home with you' definitely applied to me on numerous occasions.

I remember one particular time, which made me laugh, when I was downstairs in the practice, one December evening, putting up Christmas decorations in the front window. It was around 11:00 p.m. (I know, I know!), and a lady went walking by. She saw me, took a double take and came back and then tried to push open the practice's front door. Having no luck with that, she then mouthed to me through the glass, "Are you open?"

Incredible! Now do remember, this was 1986!

Anyway, back to Monday morning…

Eileen was in the practice when I came down. She was a lovely lady in her early 50s.

When I first began working here, she was introduced to me rather officially as Mrs Shaw. Even the owner of the opticians practice always referred to her by her surname.

I think it continued with me for about a week, if that…and then I asked her if she would mind if I dropped the Mrs Shaw bit, and she indicated that she would be more than happy if I did.

She was a very wise woman, and very knowledgeable, and I would often find myself in the position where she would be advising me in my somewhat exaggerated, busy private life. But her approach was never preaching or condescending. It was always very light-hearted and fun, and what she did say was always good food for thought anyway.

We had a doctor testing just for the morning, with patients booked every 20 minutes, and the time absolutely flew by. Eileen had the post to do, the clinic paperwork and various phone calls, as well as dealing with people arriving for their appointments. And I was dispensing every Tom, Dick and Harriet; and by 1:00 p.m. (when we closed for lunch), we were ready for the break and looking forward to the hopeful calmness of the afternoon to get organised again.

The doctor had left to go home, Eileen had gone out to do some shopping, and I had just closed the practice side-door to go up to the flat to get myself something to eat.

As I walked towards the concrete stairway, I heard a rather fast moving Jackie descending, and I moved to one side to wait until she reached the bottom. She was on her way over to the health food store to do the afternoon shift…and she was late!

I jokingly said I needed a lie down as we'd been so busy.

She gave me one of her vague looks as she hurried by, saying, "Oh wow…I thought you'd been in your flat…glad you're OK anyway…see you later."

"Yeah, see you soon…have a good time at work," I said, with a rather puzzled tone to my voice, as I watched her continuing her dash to the front door.

That was odd…what did she mean by that?

I started to walk up the concrete stairs…thinking…

A few months ago, I was in the flat, one Saturday afternoon, listening to some music in the living room, when some lad practically walked all the way up the stairs, stopped and then looked at me…with a startled look on his face.

Initially I thought he was a friend of Jackie's, so thinking he'd come in the wrong door, I informed him so and said that she was out, working at the moment. It then became obvious that he hadn't come in the wrong door, as he ran back down the stairs like a man possessed, with me chasing after him as I watched him leap over our back wall and then over the wall behind the wine bar.

Jackie and I always used to leave our flat doors unlocked; but from that incident onwards, we thought better of it as we

27

didn't realise that people could access the flats from behind the opticians practice.

I walked up to my door, put the key in and turned it…phew, it unlocked. I was pretty sure I had locked it earlier, but what Jackie had said had given me the impression that she'd thought she'd heard somebody in my flat…

I started to walk up the staircase and even though I knew the door had been locked, I still felt a bit uneasy.

I got to the top and walked out onto the living room floor.

There was no one here. Of course there was no one here, how could there be, but I still had a very strange feeling.

The atmosphere of the flat felt different somehow…

I wanted to check the rooms.

Goodness knows what I was expecting to find, but I went into my bedroom, came back out and then went down the corridor into the kitchen, putting my head in the bathroom on the way and then walked back to the living room again.

There was definitely no one here…I had convinced myself! But the place really did feel different.

I turned on the disco deck and put on a record and then walked back down to the kitchen.

I made a sandwich and returned to the living room and sat down on the sofa. I still kept looking around. It was very strange; the flat just seemed odd, but I couldn't understand why.

I ate most of my sandwich and then went back down to the kitchen again. I stopped halfway along the corridor and turned the light on in the bathroom and looked inside again.

What was going on? What was I doing? It was lunchtime, it was broad daylight and sunny, I had music playing; yet I just felt very uneasy, and I couldn't understand why!

The bathroom looked as it had looked ten minutes ago; and of course, it would do! I don't know why I had to peer inside again, but I just felt the need to do so.

The window openings in the flat were all closed at the back, and they were all positioned high up anyway and out of reach. The living/dining room part of the flat always seemed to keep a nice, even, comfortable temperature in the summer, so I never felt the need to open any of them.

The only two windows I did open occasionally were in my bedroom and the kitchen, and they were two floors up above the road!

But I couldn't help it; I just kept thinking that there was someone else in here with me.

THERE IS NO ONE HERE OK…JUST ME!

I turned off the music and went back downstairs. I fancied a quick walk outside before we opened up the practice again.

I didn't mention any of this to Eileen when I saw her.

I must admit, I actually had it on my mind; but for some reason, I didn't say anything.

I never went straight up to the flat that night after we'd finished work (and that wasn't unusual), but instead I went around to the local Indian restaurant. I used to go there, or the wine bar next door, and have a meal. I would sit there with my *Evening Standard* newspaper and a half pint of lager (sounds very old mannish I know), and I would do that three or four times a week I guess. Now I know that probably comes over as rather extravagant, but remember I lived on my own; I had no ties and no big bills, so why not.

Eileen would always say that I should eat-in more and save my money, but I didn't ALWAYS act on her advice!

I'd sit there reading the paper but not really reading it; if you know what I mean.

I was like a patient in a dentist's waiting room (or an optician's), flicking through the magazines. It rested my mind, that's all, and I used it as relaxing and winding-down time, and I really looked forward to this at the end of a busy day.

It's funny you know, but I'd normally always see the same two or three other chaps in the Indian restaurant as well. They'd be sitting on their own, like me, reading a newspaper or a book. We all reservedly acknowledged each other, but we never spoke. It was like a little silent club.

The meal was superb, but I did fancy another drink and of 'proper' lager this time as well. The Indian only ever served their version, which I felt was never as nice as 'pub' lager, so I walked across the road and into the Three Tuns public house, or as I used to call it the 'Three Tuns of Fun.' Mind you, that was definitely said with tongue-in-cheek!

This was the pub where the local traders would often frequent…so of course, this is where you would always find me! (Cough, cough.)

The landlord in there was a man called Charlie. He was your real typical London landlord with a stocky round build and rosy cheeks. He used to call me Stevie, which always made me smile.

Occasionally, I would go in there at lunchtime too on my own or with a frame rep, and that's when Charlie would demonstrate his methods of trying to get you to come back in the evening; which, to be honest, I never really cottoned on to, until I'd moved away from the town. It worked like this…

When you were about to leave to go back to work, he'd notice you might still have a fair amount of drink left in your glass, so he'd come over and offer to put cling film over the top and store it behind the bar, so that you could return later on that evening to finish it off!

Now, I know that you're probably thinking, YUCK! But I'll tell you something…it worked…it tasted absolutely fine and still amazingly fresh, and it also worked for Charlie too because it DID bring me back later!

…and there was always a group of other cling-filmed beer glasses, sitting there behind the bar alongside mine; all with names scrawled on bits of paper that sat underneath them…so it wasn't just me falling for his tactics!

I'll tell you something else; Charlie had a superb memory. About a year or so after I had moved away, I returned for a birthday bash that was taking place in the town. And to use up some time before going to the do, I went into the Three Tuns for old time's sake for a drink. He soon spotted me and came over, and, to my amazement, said, "Same as usual, Stevie?" …incredible!

Anyway, I'm digressing again…sorry…back to '86!

I ordered a pint of Tennant's lager, with a top of lemonade, and sat down with my newspaper. Tennant's top was my tipple in the Tuns (try saying that after a few!)…I was also partial to their Golden Glow peanuts, which were sold there in the smallest size packets you ever did see. A couple of shakes into the palm of your hand, and they'd be gone. They were lovely though, and although I was fairly full up with the Indian, I could always still find some room for a packet or two…terrible I know.

It was just starting to get dusk outside around 9:30 p.m. as I left the pub and walked around to the practice, stopping to look into the front window at our window display.

Hmm, that 'frame of the month' idea was wearing a bit thin now, especially as I had put it in there at the beginning of May!

I punched in the key code on the side door; and after pressing in the good old light plunger, I made my way along the corridor. At the end, just to one side of the concrete stairs, was the storeroom. I unlocked it, went in and turned on the light. I was keeping my old Honda CB200 motorbike inside, which I was attempting to restore.

I stood there looking at it for a few minutes…(dreaming). I was making progress with the makeover albeit quite slow. But I knew I'd definitely have it on the road, looking all shiny and new one day.

I came out, turning off the light, and I shut the door.

Would you believe it! The corridor light was still on…it had a mind of its own!

I started to walk up the concrete stairs to the flat, pushing in the second light plunger at the top for good measure.

I was turning different things over in my mind as I walked through…*I'd better phone my parents and see how they are, especially as it's been 'my turn' to phone for a while now, hmm, but perhaps I'll get some music on and have a soak in the bath first; mind you they do go to bed early, so maybe I should phone them first instead…*

As I got to the hallway, I noticed Jackie's light on through the glass above her door; and without hesitation, I knocked. She came out almost immediately.

"Steveeeeee!" she said as if she hadn't seen me for years, and we gave each other a big hug.

"Did you get told off for being late?" I asked, "I've never seen you moving so fast."

We had a laugh and a chat, and she beckoned me in, but I knew that would involve more drink, and I had work in the morning, AND that disco bath was calling out, so I thanked her but declined her offer.

31

We had another hug, said goodnight, and I unlocked my door.

I turned on the light switch inside and started to walk up the stairs.

As I reached the top, I stopped dead in my tracks!

The first thing I saw was the cushion from the sofa lying on the floor.

I went over and turned on the main living room light and realised that the sofa was actually sticking out at an angle from the wall.

I reacted with a loud "HEY!" that was said in a rather nervous manner as my eyes danced all around the room…

Talk about sobering up fast!

Was there someone in here?

I reached out quickly and switched on the bedroom light and looked inside.

What was going on? I may've forgotten about the spoon, but I KNOW I didn't leave the cushion there…and as for the sofa!

My bedroom looked normal.

I flicked on the kitchen light switch; and after waiting for the fluorescent tube to decide to work, I made my way cautiously down the corridor.

I pushed open the bathroom door quickly and pulled the light cord…then after satisfying myself that there was no one in there, I walked with further trepidation down to the kitchen.

…there was no one there either!

I walked fast back up the corridor and looked around the living room area, and then I went back into the bedroom and opened up the wardrobe doors…ridiculous I know, but I had to convince myself.

…I was definitely alone…thank goodness!

I felt relieved, but still really nervous…what the heck was going on?

I picked up the cushion and looked over at the sofa…

My God! It was a good two feet away from the wall at one end. How on EARTH?

I pushed it back against the wall with my knee and then stood still and slowly looked around the living room and over to the dining table area…

Then, I looked down at the cushion in my hands.

"Come on you bloody thing, tell me what happened…how did you end up on the floor?"

I edged myself slowly down on to the sofa and sat there looking around.

I just didn't know what to think.

I must've sat there for a good five minutes, which doesn't sound long, but it is when your mind is whirring around at 100mph, trying to fathom out what had just transpired!

I finally got up and went down to the kitchen to make a drink.

I could hear Jackie's music playing below, which was certainly a comforting sound indeed, as I switched on the kettle to make some coffee.

I stood there leaning against the sink as I contemplated what had taken place again.

Perhaps I had a ghost?

"Are you a ghost?" I said out loud as I leaned forward and looked back up the corridor to the living room, as if expecting a reply.

Blimey, now I'm really going mad.

I took my coffee and walked back up the corridor and placed it on the dining table. I pulled up a chair and sat down. My eyes were scanning around the room again, but my main gaze was towards the sofa.

Something had pulled the damn thing out from the wall at one end…there was no other explanation!

I sat there staring and thinking.

My mind was spinning with possible causes, ranging from the something natural to the something supernatural…boy oh boy, this was crazy.

I went to bed, giving my planned disco bath the miss.

I was constantly churning things over in my mind, but thankfully, I fell asleep; and amazingly, I slept like a log. I did briefly wake up around 3:00 a.m., with the radio still on, but that wasn't unusual as I would often fall asleep with the radio playing quietly in the background.

I had a wooden stool to the side of the bed, near the window, which was my makeshift bedside table; and upon this stood my radio and my alarm clock. I'd knocked the radio onto the floor the other night in my sleepy attempt to turn it off, but it still seemed to be working OK.

Tuesday, June 17th
Atmospheric Pressure

The next morning, I got out of bed and went immediately into the living room and looked at the sofa. It was on my mind as soon as I awoke. Thankfully, it hadn't moved overnight, and I went into the bathroom and turned on the taps to run a bath. As I brushed my teeth, I kept checking the hot water as it did have a tendency to suddenly go cold rather quickly. But it kept amazingly hot this time, and I ended up turning it off in the end and leaving the cold tap running to cool the bath water down.

...And I deliberately left the bathroom door wide open when I got in the bath. It just felt better somehow.

After my bath, I went around to the airing cupboard and switched off the hot water tank timer. I wasn't too concerned with domestic money savings, and I don't mean that because I was well off, but I knew that I had hardly used any hot water because it WAS so hot; and in my mind, I was sure that I'd have more than enough hot water for tonight. I just had to make sure I remembered to turn the thing back on for tomorrow though!

After a slice of toast, I went downstairs to the practice, just before 8:30 a.m. and did my normal work preparations. I had gone down a bit earlier than normal today as I had arranged with a frame rep to call on me before we opened the practice, so that it didn't interfere with the business too much. I also felt good getting out of the flat anyway and was thinking, as I walked down the stairs, that I wouldn't be looking forward to going back up again at lunchtime.

Carla was working today, and I had her coffee poured out and sitting ready on the desk in the back office as usual. She liked it black, and I always said to her that by the time she'd arrive, it would have cooled down enough to be the right temperature to drink. She never complained either way, but then Carla probably wouldn't.

Just before 8:45, the rep was knocking on the door; and Carla and I never managed to really speak properly until around 10:00 a.m.

She asked me how the wedding reception went; and to be honest, I had to really think hard for the answer, as the flat shenanigans were now dominating my mind.

For some reason though, I didn't want to tell Carla about the flat. Whether it was male pride and not wanting to actually admit that I was worried, or whether it was because it all sounded too daft to be true? I don't know. Whatever it was, I didn't say anything to her.

Lunchtime soon came.

Carla had treated me to a sandwich, which she insisted that I had to eat in the back office with her. She was off on holiday to Devon in her caravan tomorrow for the rest of the week, and she wanted to chat. It was the first time she'd ever bought me lunch too…and it was almost like she knew that I didn't want to go back upstairs!

The afternoon was quite busy; and before you knew it, it was soon 5:30 p.m. The last patient had left just before 5:00 p.m., which enabled us to get all end of day stuff completed and out of the way, and we finished dead on time.

Eileen and Carla would always leave by the way of the side practice door when we had closed, and I would always escort them down the passageway to the front. I don't know why…it just seemed the right thing to do I guess, like a gesture of thanks for their hard work throughout the day. Anyway, it became a bit of a habit for me, and I almost felt bad if I didn't do it.

Carla walked ahead of me down the corridor.

"Now just you behave yourself while I'm away!" she said as she opened the door.

"I think I should be saying that to you!" I replied, with a laugh.

She turned back to look at me with a smile on her face… "Chance would be a fine thing."

We said our goodbyes; and after wishing her a great holiday, I shut the door and made my way upstairs to the flat.

I've got to be honest…I was really dreading this now.

It was almost like the trepidation had doubled because I hadn't gone up at lunchtime. It's funny how the mind works.

Oh blimey, what would I find this time…?

I opened the flat door and walked apprehensively up the stairs.

I could sense the different atmosphere again even before I reached the top.

It was sort of heavy and muffled, creating an almost closed in type feeling. It felt really strange. I walked out onto the living room floor and looked around.

Everything thankfully was where it should be. I checked the bedroom, bathroom and the kitchen, and again all was fine.

Thank goodness for that!

There was just this strange dull heavy atmosphere, like everything was wrapped in cotton wool; it was very odd.

I sat down on the sofa. My eyes were scanning the walls from top to bottom and mainly in the corners. Goodness knows why as it seemed quite an exaggerated thing to do, but it felt reassuring that everything looked how it should be everywhere…and I mean everywhere.

The place just wasn't right though, and deep down I knew I wasn't right either.

I didn't feel my normal relaxed self. I was on edge. I felt pensive, and I knew that I wouldn't normally be doing some of the things that I was now doing.

As soon as I walked onto the living room floor, I would have usually put on some music and started dancing around. But here I was…sitting…listening…almost expecting something to happen as I scrutinised everything.

After a while, I got up and went into the bedroom and changed out of my work clothes. I had to do something; this was all driving me mad. I went into the bathroom and turned on the bath taps. Two baths in one day! Now that certainly wouldn't have been allowed if I'd been living at home!

I've always said that I do my best thinking in the bath, and I still reckon that's true to this day.

The water came out incredibly hot almost straight away, and I immediately thought of the water tank. I knew the water timer was off, but like I said earlier, I hadn't used much hot water; so I should have enough left for a shallow bath. I turned off the cold tap though just in case, dropped in some bath salts; and with the hot water filling the bath, I came back out into the living room.

I turned on the television (which sat on yet another stool) behind the far end of the sofa. It was a 15-inch Grundig colour TV set that I'd won in a spectacle frame dispensing competition last year. I'd dispensed specs for England to win it too!

I went to the airing cupboard and took out a bath towel, then I stood watching a bit of TV until that inner warning alarm goes off, reminding you of something…in this case…the running bath water!

I went back into the bathroom and put my hand under the tap…blimey, I pulled it back rather sharpish…it was still coming out absolutely baking hot…! There was still loads of hot water left. I turned it off and turned on the cold tap. I liked a hot bath but not THAT hot.

I would frequently bring my cassette tape player into the bathroom and blast the walls with recorded disco music when I had a bath, but tonight I just didn't feel like it. I also deliberately pushed the bathroom door wide open again, like this morning. The feeling of not wanting to be shut in was quite strong once more. Mind you, I couldn't see anything outside the bathroom though, other than the kitchen corridor wall, but somehow just being able to see outside of the four walls seemed to make me feel better. I'm not claustrophobic, and I'd always normally close the door. But I just needed that 'open' spacey feel for some reason at the moment. I think that's why I didn't want any music in there with me either… I wanted to be able to hear everything that was going on outside the bathroom too.

I lay there in the bath thinking for a bit, with the distant sounds of the TV in the background…

The bath was parallel to the corridor wall, and I kept turning my head to the right and looking at the plain, fawn-coloured wood-chipped wall.

I started leaning back slightly…how far could I see down the passageway?

Oh, this was daft… I just couldn't relax… I felt so uneasy, I felt like something was going to pop its head around the door frame any minute! PLEASE NO!

I was listening past the noise of the TV, sitting motionless in the bath, staring and concentrating, not moving a muscle…trying to project my hearing into the living room…

RIGHT! I'm not having this!

This was getting ridiculous.

I quickly washed myself over and got out of the bath and dried myself down in the bedroom. It was a relief to get out of the bathroom. I put on some shorts and a T-shirt and went into the kitchen and put the kettle on to make some tea.

I stood there thinking again…

I started turning over in my mind what had recently taken place in the flat.

The spoon on the floor…the cushion and the sofa…the changed atmosphere…

…And then, I recalled the slap on the arm… Blimey, I'd forgotten about that…was that connected with all this too?

It could be…but was I just putting two and two together and making a worrying five? Did the slap on the arm thing really happen?

Of course, it bloody did; I'd had a red mark on my skin, and it stung!

But the more I thought about it, I began doubting myself. There may've been a logical explanation, but I certainly couldn't come up with anything.

I know it DID happen, and it was a physical occurrence too…and that made it even scarier if it was all part of everything else that was going on.

I poured out my tea and went back into the living room.

I turned off the TV and laid down on the sofa, putting my mug on the floor, and then put the cushion behind my head on the sofa arm.

I was thinking too much. I was driving myself mad trying to make sense of all the weirdness that was going on.

I can't say that I've ever thought about the reality of ghosts and the like. I've certainly never had any experiences of one anyway.

Could this be what was happening now?

It certainly would explain a few things if 'explain' was the right word to use.

I sat forward, as if meaning business; and in my mind, I did.

I was going to start dealing with this differently. I needed to try and change my mindset with what was taking place. I knew my behaviour had altered, and I didn't like it.

Perhaps there WAS something in my flat that was doing all this, but I had to deal with it and not let it get to me.

Right! I got up and went over to the disco unit and turned it on...

Wednesday, June 18th
In Hot Water

I woke up at just before 3:00 a.m. again. The radio was still on, with a man talking the night away.

I leaned over and turned it off and then lay there listening to the silence.

It's always amazing what you think you can hear when there really isn't anything to hear. I was straining every sinew, trying to project my hearing awareness as far as I could, just like I did in the bathroom earlier.

I turned over and looked into the blackness that was the living room.

Come on…for goodness' sake, let's get back to sleep.

I lay there for a further few minutes, and then I must have dozed back off again.

It was a quiet Wednesday at work, and I had loads of time talking with Eileen. I decided to forget about my male pride this time, and I told her about what was happening in the flat, and she listened intently.

She asked me if I had mentioned any of it to Carla; and when I said that I hadn't, she intimated that I should; as she felt that Carla would almost certainly have an interest.

Eileen also came up with the idea of perhaps contacting the last tenant, a lady called Janet who was actually my managerial predecessor, just to see whether she may have had any similar experiences. Mind you, I must admit, I more or less dismissed that immediately as I was sure that Janet would've said something to Eileen and Carla anyway if something odd had been going on.

Eileen then additionally mentioned our boss Mr Barnes, who was also my landlord too, and said that I should perhaps have a chat with him as well; as for all we know, he may have documented historical information pertaining to the strange goings on at his fingertips.

I felt good telling Eileen.

She was a good listener, and she always gave me other angles and outlets to my somewhat blinkered thinking.

I certainly felt easier about the whole situation too. She also reinforced my thoughts that I wasn't going to allow this thing, whatever it was, to interfere with my normal day-to-day living in the flat.

It was playing on my mind all the time though, so this was going to be easier said than done.

After work, I went straight upstairs to the flat. I had it on my mind that I was going to make some tea, listen to some music for a bit and then FINALLY get around to phoning my parents.

As I opened the door and walked up the stairs, I instantaneously said out loud, "Hi, how're doing…? Have you had a good day?"

It just came out… I don't know why… It was just a new reaction to the situation I suppose.

Thankfully, no one replied!

Strangely, I did feel a lot better for saying it though.

It was like it had given me the edge, as if I was in control now…like I was now accepting that it was here and was just getting on with it all. It certainly made me feel a lot calmer anyway.

Perhaps it was the Eileen influence again.

The horrible dull atmosphere was very present, and I realised that it always seemed more obvious when I had returned to the flat from work or after I'd been out. As I said before, it was really quite difficult to describe the feeling properly, as it WAS just a feeling. It was nothing visual, thank goodness, and I suppose I was getting used to it I guess or at least trying to…and phew, everything was where it had been this morning, as I surveyed the living and dining area. Again, I was expecting something to have been moved, but I still did a quick scout around the rest of the flat to be sure.

I took off my work gear, put some casual stuff on and then went into the kitchen to make some beans on toast. That was about my cooking limit when I stayed in.

I ate my tea at the table rather rapidly and then took my empty plate into the kitchen. My bowl and mug were there from this morning, and I turned on the taps to wash them up.

The hot water came out boiling again, literally scalding.

The hot water tank is off…I know it's off…it cannot STILL be this hot surely…

I went to the airing cupboard; and sure enough, everything was off. I felt the tank… WOW, it was absolutely baking hot and feeling it with my bare hands did rather concern me, as I'd never actually felt it this hot before.

Coincidentally, the electrician that the landlord uses was coming into the practice tomorrow to fit an extra plug socket in the back office. I think it'll be a good idea to ask him if he wouldn't mind coming up to have a look at this as well… I'm sure Mr Barnes would rather I did anyway.

I washed up and made myself a mug of tea and then went back into the living room.

I turned on the disco unit, put on a LP record and then lay full-length on the sofa.

I was propped up on the cushion as I sipped about half of my tea; then as I placed the mug down on the carpet, I puffed up the cushion behind me to get more comfy.

I lay there relaxing and listening to the music for about ten minutes, and I was dozing slightly as I slowly closed and opened my eyes…

Bloody hell! What was that?

I was fully awake in an instant, turning my head immediately and sharply to look fully to the right as I urgently swung my legs to the floor in one fast sweeping move, kicking my mug over with my feet, sending the remaining tea spilling out onto the carpet and under the sofa.

Out of the corner of my eye, I'd seen a dark figure on the stairs!

I sat bolt upright and stared at the stairwell for a second…then jumped up and went over to look further down.

There was nothing there!

Boy, oh boy, that happened so quick! …did I really see something?

I kept looking down the stairwell.

Was it just a reflection from my glasses?

Blimey, it seemed a whole lot more real than that to me, but there was definitely nothing there.

I kept looking down the stairs…my eyes darting from the top to the bottom…and then I looked back at the sofa and then down at the tea…that was soaking itself into the carpet…arghhh!

I ran out into the kitchen and got a floor cloth from under the sink and rinsed it out under the tap, then ran back and picked up the mug and put it on the dining table as I started to rub the cloth into the carpet, trying to soak up as much as I could of the spilt tea whilst keeping an eye on the stairs.

I made a couple of journeys back and forth to the kitchen until I had made best of the spillage, and then I returned to the sofa; and after observing the stairs again…I sat back.

I started to try and make the image appear in my specs…perhaps it HAD just been a reflection.

I moved my head slowly up and down, like a nodding dog, as I looked straight ahead at the window; then I turned my eyes to look sideways at the stairs through my spec lenses. I immediately compared it with the efforts that I had made after the slap on the arm on Saturday, when I tried to make that happen again too.

There was a bit of reflection, but nothing that produced the horrible dark image that I saw before.

Man alive, what is going on now… It's getting to be one thing after another!

Is it me imagining these things, getting carried away with it all? It could be I suppose…I just don't know.

I sat there, feeling really uneasy again.

Now come on, Steve, for goodness' sake; you said that you weren't going to let this get to you anymore!

Right! I've got to occupy my mind.

I headed purposely down the stairs to the practice… I'm definitely going to phone my parents!

I had no phone in the flat, so I used the one in the practice in the back office.

I didn't feel I was taking advantage of Mr Barnes doing this, as I only ever really used it on the odd occasion to keep in touch with my family…and he did know anyway.

I spoke to my parents, but I never told them about the fuss in the flat. I wanted too; but if I had of done, I know I would have had my mother phoning the practice every day to check if I was alright!

I did mention to my father though about the boiler, as he was an electrician by trade. He just stated the obvious, saying that I must have left something switched on somewhere. But I knew for sure that everything was off.

I went for a walk after the phone call and ended up in the Three Tuns, as I fancied a sit down somewhere AWAY from the flat.

I got myself a drink and found a seat.

I heard one of the patrons say, "Where's the big fella tonight?"

"Charlie is upstairs, having a lie down; he's not feeling well," replied one of the bar staff.

"Go and tell him that it doesn't feel the same without him down here," someone else piped up.

…and that was true.

The whole atmosphere was different without his cheery face and voice. He made the place. It was the sort of pub that never really got heaving with people, so I guess that made his extrovert presence stand out even more.

As I sat there drinking, I thought of the similarity to the flat.

The atmosphere was SO different in there too, only no one had left…more like some THING had arrived!

The local dentist and his wife were at the bar, and they gave me a wave that indicated their intentions of wanting to come over and join me… I beckoned them to do so but with reservation in my thoughts, as I knew what I was probably letting myself in for. They were the sort of people that always talked 'shop'; and on previous occasions with them, I had always tried to interject some diverse comment now and then in an effort to lighten and change the direction of the conversation; and initially tonight, I could see it going the same way. As the evening progressed though, they seemed much less intent on 'work' chat; and in the end, I saw them in a completely different light, and I must say I really did enjoy their company.

We all walked out laughing together at closing time, said goodnight, and I ambled back around to the practice.

I was in quite a joyful merry mood when I unlocked my front door; and as I turned on the lights, I practically ran up the stairs, with a totally unconcerned attitude.

I stood on the living room floor and greeted the flat in a rather somewhat theatrical manner.

I really couldn't give two monkeys tonight…

I looked over at the table and saw the mug was lying on its side.

Did I leave it like that? I'm sure I didn't. Did I knock it over in my haste to clean up the carpet? Of course, I did not!

I picked it up and looked at it, expecting it to magically tell me what had happened.

The cushion never did, so I guess the mug wouldn't either!

But at this merry moment in time, I didn't really care.

I put the tape player on, and I had a little dance around for a while until sleep and drink started to take its toll, and I thought I'd better call it a day. And after wishing the flat a good night, I turned everything off, climbed into bed, and I must have fallen asleep practically straight away.

Thursday, June 19th
Doesn't Sound Good

I woke up rather sharply. It was almost like my body had said, "WAKE UP!"

It was still dark, and I lay there for a few moments, thinking why I had woken up with such a start. I leaned over for the alarm clock to see the time…it had just gone 3:00 a.m. AGAIN.

I licked my lips and realised how dry they were, and how incredibly thirsty I was, and I had just started to make an effort to get out of bed to get some water…when…

CREAK…CREAK…CREAK…CREAK…it was the kitchen corridor!

Someone was walking down the bloody kitchen corridor!

The unanticipated sudden break in the silence was earth-shattering, and I shouted out with a reactionary panic-stricken "HEY!" as I jumped out of bed, like a sprinter from the blocks, grabbed my specs and put them on and then ran into the living room. I whacked the main light switch on; and after scanning the living room around me, I stood with adrenaline pumping, staring down the dimly lit kitchen corridor and was ridiculously leaning to one side, as if trying not to show myself.

I then quickly moved to the corridor wall and whacked on the kitchen light. It was that ruddy, slow-starting fluorescent tube which made a 'dong-dong' type sound as the starter motor tried to kick it into action. The tube was flashing on and off, on and off, like a slow strobe, as I tried to focus… "Come on! Come on!" And then suddenly, 'ping'; the kitchen was ablaze with seemingly pure white light as I squinted to adjust to its brightness.

NOTHING! …there was no one there.

I edged down to the bathroom…I was really pumped up…

"COME OUT!"I shouted.

I stood back slightly to one side of the door, like an armed policeman waiting for shots to fire out from an assailant within, then I banged open the door with the side of my fist!

"COME OUT!" I shouted again, and then I grabbed the light cord and pulled on the light…

NOTHING!

Blimey, I was shaking…and my chest was pounding like a drum!

I walked quickly back into the living room, with the kitchen corridor floor creaking under my every step.

That was DEFINITELY the noise I had heard.

I stood perfectly still like a statue…my panic was lessening as I thankfully realised I was alone.

It was completely quiet.

I was listening to see if I could hear Jackie moving downstairs.

I'm not sure whether I would've been able to hear her anyway, but I was certain I must've woken her up with the amount of noise I'd been making with all the running around and shouting.

I stood there listening, but all remained perfectly quiet.

I sat down on the edge of the sofa.

Blimey, I was relieved, but I was still shaking.

I was looking around the flat again.

Right…there was definitely no other person in here other than me, but I SO thought that there was!

I'M COMPLETELY ON MY OWN, OK? COMPLETELY!

I exhaled a long breath of air in further relief…*THIS IS CRAZY!*

I got up and walked over to the stairs, then walked down a couple of steps and leaned over the bannister so I could see through the glass over the top of my front door. I often did this in the evening to see whether Jackie was in, as her light would shine through into the hallway.

Well, I knew that she was in, and hopefully I hadn't awoken her as all was still dark.

I stood on the living room floor. I felt scared, but at the same time, I felt angry. I was clenching my fists as I went over and sat back down on the sofa and looked around again.

I really had felt that there was someone in here; that someone had somehow broken in.

But there was no one else here…there was just me.

I got up and walked back into the bedroom and sat on the bed thinking. What had caused the creaking sounds then? Could it have been the floorboards expanding or contracting? …pah! Who am I trying to kid? They were definitely footsteps. They were DEFINITELY bloody footsteps!

Oh God, I'm never going to get to sleep now, I'm so wide awake and so on edge…and still SO thirsty!

I went back down into the kitchen and poured myself a glass of water and then stood there having a drink, as I tuned in to a car speeding down the road outside. I stood perfectly still and focused on the sound as it roared through the town; its engine noise changing as it decreased and increased its speed on and off and into the distance. I had my head cocked to one side as I directed the sound through the window and curtains and into my straining ears until I was sure I could hear it no more…then I walked up the kitchen corridor; and after turning off the lights, I climbed back into bed.

I then lay there…listening…listening…listening…

I've got to get back to sleep…

I awoke next to the sound of my alarm. I hadn't done that for ages. I would always wake up just before it sounded, even if I'd had a few drinks the night before.

It was 7:45 a.m.

I jumped out of bed and got ready for work.

Phew, what a night! …that was so scary.

Everything seemed OK in the flat, and there was nothing moved or out of place as I swiftly had some toast, got ready for work and made my way downstairs to the practice.

It had just gone 8:30 a.m., and Eileen was already in the back office, and was putting the kettle on as I opened the side door.

She immediately started speaking eagerly, saying that she'd spoken with Mr Barnes and that he'd said that nothing had ever been mentioned by any other tenant about any strange occurrences in the flat before.

I thanked her for enquiring about it for me (good old Eileen), and then I told her of my early morning experiences.

We sat there talking about it all until we were interrupted by a knocking on the practice's front door. It was Dr Johnson, who was here to do the morning clinic…oh blimey, it had gone 9:00 a.m.!

The morning went by quickly; and at lunchtime, Eileen reminded me again that I should definitely tell Carla, when she was back on Monday, about all the flat antics. It made me smile as I was starting to think of Carla as some kind of exorcist.

The afternoon was very quiet, with no sight testing going on. The 'entertainment' was the electrician, who called in to fit the new plug socket. He was the sort of chap that would keep trying to crack jokes all the time, which is fine to a point; but after a while, he had PASSED that point with both me and Eileen, and we had to come away and leave him to it.

Eileen made me laugh when she said that she was going to offer him a cup of tea, but then she changed her mind…

I had brought up the subject of the incredibly hot water tank in the flat though, and he said that he'd take a look after he'd fitted the new socket. Eileen said that she'd call the ghost busters if we didn't come back down in ten minutes! Thankfully, he didn't hear.

I walked in front of him up the stairs and onto the living room floor. I looked at his face as I pointed to the airing cupboard. His expression and body language remained the same. I was hoping he might say something about the muffled atmosphere, but he made no comment at all.

He had a good look at the boiler and did blaspheme on how hot it was, and he couldn't believe that I hadn't had the immersion heater on or the normal timer on for days, adding that the temperature of the water suggested that I had only just turned the immersion off!

Well, I hadn't had anything turned on since Tuesday morning!

It was quite obvious though from his tone of voice that he didn't believe what I was saying, as he kept saying that the immersion must have only just been turned off (for what reason I would do that I do NOT know), but I guess I would be doubting things too in his shoes if I was being presented with this sort of situation.

"Perhaps the fairies are turning it on and off when you're not looking," he said, with a sarcastic smile.

Yes, thank you for that!

I asked if he would confirm that there wasn't any power going into the tank at the moment, to which he agreed.

"Everything is off," he said deliberately, and then he raised his eyebrows as he turned and glanced at me with a look of scepticism.

I really did not like this man.

As we walked back down the corridor to the front door, he turned to me and quipped…

"Looks like you're going to be getting FAIRY cheap electricity bills then…!"

I ALMOST smiled!

I told Eileen what he'd said about the boiler (not his joke), and she reckoned that I should phone the electricity company anyway, just at least to report it and also to make sure that the charges would be correct.

Hmmm, like I said before, I didn't do everything she suggested…

We said goodbye just after 5:30 p.m., and I locked up the practice and made my way up to the flats.

I knocked on Jackie's door.

She greeted me with her normal enthusiasm and invited me inside, asking me if I was hungry. Well, I certainly didn't have to think twice about that tonight, I was sort of hoping that she would ask me anyway. I wanted to tell Jackie about what was happening upstairs and to apologise about the noise from the night before too.

She put some music on, and we sat down on the carpet with our backs against the wall. Jackie gave me a single fork and a potato in a dessert bowl, and we tucked in.

Her potatoes were legendary amongst her friends. She would bake them, take out the potato pulp, mix it with whatever Jackie mixed it with (cough cough), and then put it all back in again. She'd then wrap them in baking foil and keep them warm in the oven. WOW, I'll tell you, they were lovely, so creamy…and so tasty.

Jackie looked at me with her normal faraway look in her eyes as I told her of the past few nights. She carried on eating, but occasionally let out an 'Oh wowww'…and an 'Oh mannn'.

I apologised about the noise from last night, mentioning how the 'walking' on the creaky kitchen corridor had scared the living daylights out of me, but she said that she had been oblivious to it all.

The only real noises she said she ever heard from me upstairs sometimes WERE the creaky floorboards and my music. She said she quite liked to hear the music too because it made her feel that she was not alone in the building.

…and that made me think back to last Monday when I had caught her rushing down the stairs on the way to work. She had commented that she'd thought I'd been in the flat during the morning…what had she heard? Was it the creaky floorboards then too?

Well, unfortunately it was, and she added that it had sounded like I was walking back and forth like a 'caged lion'…in fact, she went on to say that she was on the verge of knocking on my door to check on me because she thought that there might have been something wrong!

"Oh mannn!" (That was me saying it this time!)

I definitely needed a beer, but Jackie had pre-empted the situation and had already got up to get us both one!

We continued sitting on the floor, talking and drinking, until it started to get dark.

We talked about many things, but our conversation kept returning to the presence upstairs in my flat. And I did regard it as a presence now. Something was definitely up there with me.

I was standing in our walkway between the flats, wishing Jackie goodnight just before midnight. I thanked her for the food and drink, and we gave each other a big hug as always. She stood and waited until I unlocked my door, and then I turned to her and said with a big smile, "Do you wanna come up and meet the ghost?"

Jackie closed her eyes and shook her head slowly from side to side.

It's funny, you know, because thinking about it now, for the whole four or five years I lived there, I cannot recall Jackie ever coming up to my flat! It was strange really because I was often in hers.

We parted company, and I turned on the light and walked up the stairs. I greeted the flat as I reached the top, and then I went over and turned on the main light.

Good, nothing looked out of place.

I turned on the kitchen light too and walked through to the flickering of the tube. The floor creaked as normal under my weight, and I immediately thought whether Jackie might have heard it. I couldn't hear any music on downstairs still, so I assumed that she probably had done...and that made me smile as her probable reactionary facial contortion was seen in my mind's eye.

Hmm, I kept thinking about Jackie's 'caged lion' expression. It's strange that she said that you know, because I've always had a fear of lions. It stems back to when I was younger. I used to have nightmares of being chased by one through corridors and rooms of a house...it was horrible. Anyway, enough of that...

I poured myself a glass of milk from the fridge and brought it back through to the living room. I then stood in front of the sofa, casually looking around, as I slowly drank. Well, I say casually...it was a little bit more premeditated than that, but I did feel quite relaxed.

I was soon in bed and lights out.

Friday, June 20th
Food for Thought

It was a normal morning routine first thing as I got out of bed and went into the bathroom to brush my teeth.

I still felt a bit easier about the situation which was a nice feeling as I put my tape player on and danced around as I got ready for work.

Did I wake up around 3:00 a.m. again? D'you know what, I cannot remember...but I think that I probably did!

I had a quick slice of toast and went downstairs to the practice.

It was just before 8:45 a.m., and Eileen hadn't arrived yet. I retrieved the 'float' from the safe and got things ready for the day. I never prepared Eileen a coffee or tea in the morning as she varied her choice so much...from tea, coffee, and sometimes just a simple glass of water. So if I was down there first, I'd wait until she arrived...and she soon did.

Immediately, she wanted to know how I was getting on with things in the flat. I said it was about the same, but that I felt easier with the situation, and I really meant it. I could feel that I was in a better state of mind, and I felt happier. I don't know why though, because the flat was still weird. But I certainly did feel more relaxed.

Even Eileen said that she could tell that I was a bit more like myself, and that made me feel good too.

Chris phoned during the day and said that he and Johnny were 'busy' for a get-together later, but he added that they'd be up the pub Saturday night instead.

I was a bit disappointed, as I had been looking forward to their company tonight, but I wasn't going anywhere over the weekend, so Saturday sounded great.

When Eileen discovered that I was staying in, she went to great lengths to convince me that I should cook a proper-job meal for myself for once, and she wrote out a list of ingredients for a 'simple' recipe that I should try. I know why she was doing this. She knew all this flat stuff had been getting me down and seeing me more like my old happy-go-lucky self, she wanted to try and keep me that way by occupying my mind with other things.

We went out together at lunchtime to a supermarket across the road to get the ingredients. (Eileen certainly wasn't taking any chances!) We bought beef mince, carrots, onions and potatoes, which all added up to Eileen's 'simple' cottage pie…far from simple from my point of view!

She was fussing around me like a mother hen, making sure that I knew what I was going to do and when I was going to do it.

She really made me laugh with her persistent enthusiasm, and she added that I should telephone her during the evening if I was having any problems and needed some help.

The working day soon came to an end; and as we finished and left by the side door of the practice, Eileen gave me an unexpected hug and said, "Make sure you do it; and remember, any problems, give me a call," and then she walked off down the passage way with me following, assuring her that I would comply.

Well! I just couldn't get out of it, could I…I definitely had to do it!

Now, this was certainly going to be a first for me; as ever since I'd lived in the flat, I'd never REALLY cooked. I'd made very basic meals, which in all honesty, was just heating single things up in saucepans and then plonking them on a plate…or on a slice of toast. My goodness, I'd never gone out deliberately to buy ingredients and followed instructions on how to cook them and make a proper meal! Almost all of my eating was done in the various restaurants in the town anyway, and I know that sounds rather spendthrift; but like I mentioned earlier, I had no commitments, and I certainly wasn't spending money that I didn't have, so why not.

…I took my 'meal' out of the back office little fridge and made my way up to the flat.

I felt the same old feelings as I walked out onto the living room floor; and as I've said before, it always seemed much more exaggerated on returning to the flat. It was just a strange, muffled, closed-in, heavy feeling...*and it's funny as I write this, because I've just been to the doctor's to have my ears syringed this morning, but I can honestly assure you that it was nothing to do with my ears at the time!*

I didn't care about the atmosphere though tonight, I still felt good; and I went straight over to the disco unit and put on a record.

I had a quick glance around the living-room. Everything seemed to be where it should be.

(I know it may sound to you like I was being paranoid with all this checking around, but I was always expecting something to have happened...I always thought I'd find something that had been moved.)

I made my way down to the kitchen and put the ingredients on the kitchen top and attached Eileen's instructions to the cupboard door above, with some Sellotape.

Right! Let's get down to business.

I opened the fridge and took out a can of lager and opened it up (priorities)...then I took it through to the bedroom and got changed.

It's funny, you know, but I still do that occasionally to this day when I come home from work. There's something about putting on your civvies after a hard day 'at the office', and then picking up a nice cold drink that is sitting there, waiting for you...old habits and all that!

I returned to the kitchen and started preparing the food.

Let's put this cooker through its paces!

I began following Eileen's instructions, and soon I had everything chopped and ready for the cooking extravaganza. I then placed a frying pan on one of the electric rings and added the mince.

I hardly had any cooking utensils, and I was looking in the drawer for something to use to 'stir' the mince with. It's going to have to be my dessert spoon…

I turned on the appropriate electric ring, and I stood there for a while, browning the mince and dancing around on the spot as I listened to the music playing in the living room.

…and then the most scariest thing EVER took place!

…and I just want to remind you what was going on before I tell you…

It's a light Friday evening.

It's warm.

Music is playing.

I'm cooking.

EVERYTHING feels good.

EVERYTHING feels happy…

…and I'm dancing and jigging around on the spot…

WHEN…

…I stopped abruptly and froze!

I shouted out, **"OH MY GODDD!"** and I threw the spoon onto the cooker top in an absolute mad panic…

I KNEW IT WAS BEHIND ME!
…SO DARK, SO TALL…
IT WAS TOWERING ABOVE ME LIKE A GIANT!

The feeling was menacingly mind-blowing!

It filled my head, my mind, my god! It felt so powerful, so strong!

I cowered forward, expecting to be hit or crushed…and then, in one fast movement, as I slightly glanced behind me, **I RAN!** I took off at full pelt up the kitchen corridor to the living room, where I stopped and span around to look back.

There was nothing there, there was no one there!

I was trembling, absolutely shaking!

Oh bloody hell, what was that all about?

I stared down the corridor…then to my right, to my left, behind me.

Nothing!

I was on my own; there was no one here.

My heart was pounding like a drum; and my body felt really taught as my muscles tensed in a panicky reaction. It was as if I was performing my best Bruce Lee physique impression in front of the mirror…and I had the shakes to go with it too.

I then became suddenly aware of the music playing on the disco unit. It was so strange, but I guess my awareness of sounds had been completely suppressed by my emotions and reaction to what had just taken place.

It seemed that the record had just that second turned itself on, but I know that the music had been playing all the time.

…and then I realised what the song was, as the title was sung almost on cue…

Night to Remember by Shalamar.

I certainly wouldn't forget this one in a flamin' hurry!

The music realisation was brief and of no relief from the immediate situation, as I quickly turned it off and then stood there staring back down into the kitchen.

Oh boy, it was quieter than quiet now…horribly quiet as my eyes were transfixed down the corridor.

I was frozen to the spot. I just couldn't stop looking towards the kitchen…

Hold on, what was that?

I could see something in the air towards the right, at the end of the corridor…like a wispy grey vapour… *Oh my god, what IS that? It looks like smoke… It **IS** smoke!*

My dinner!

I suddenly switched back into 'normal' life mode and ran down the corridor to the kitchen.

It wasn't the mince, it was the spoon! The plastic handle was burning on the cooker ring by the frying pan, where it had landed after I had thrown it in my mad panic.

I flicked it off and threw it into the sink, almost in one, rather fortunate movement, turned off the cooker ring, and then stood and stared at the empty space where the black figure had been.

It had all happened so fast and so out of the blue.

I always think of ghostly happenings as being connected with dark spooky houses; I'm sure you probably do too. The situation always seems to be cold and eerie, but this was as far from that as it could ever be!

It was warm, bright and during the day...nothing that you would ever associate with any eerie goings-on at all.

I pulled up the kitchen window slightly to let some of the smell and smoke out and then turned back to the cooker and looked at my mince sitting there in the frying pan. And then I looked up at Eileen's instructions stuck on the cupboard door. Now what did she say? If I had problems or needed any help that I should give her a call? That made me slightly smile...very slightly.

I turned around again to look behind me.

I'm going to have to get some mirrors set up on the bloody wall if I'm going to carry on...I was so nervous.

I walked back into the living room and sat down on the sofa.

I was so on edge.

This had really shaken me up.

Just sheer raw panic took over me when I ran up the corridor to get away from whatever it was.

...and I can recall another instant when that had happened to me before...

I must've been about 17 years old and was walking across a playing field with two friends in the pitch black of night. We were eating separate portions of chips, wrapped in paper, when one of my friends suddenly screamed and ran ahead, like a wild man. Me and the other lad just instantly reacted and ran screaming after him with our chips flying everywhere. The first lad was, of course, messing around, and we cursed him after a 50-yard-dash of terror when he broke down laughing.

But I can remember the absolute heart-pounding, sheer-panic reaction that I had then, and this had been just like it; only this time, something really had happened. No one was joking around here!

I sat motionless. It was so strange.

It all didn't seem real, but I knew that it was.

Remember it was daylight, it was bright, it was warm, and it wasn't quiet either as the music had been on!

Sorry to keep repeating that, but it was so odd, so like it should not be happening...but it was happening.

I got up.

There was no way I could carry on with the cooking; I just had to get out of the flat.

I grabbed some money and made my way down the stairs and out of the building.

The Three Tuns: here I come!

I went in and walked straight up to the bar and ordered a sausage and chips and a pint of Tennant's top and sat down in the corner.

I could see Charlie serving down the other end, and he gave me a wave, but I couldn't see anyone else in there that I knew.

...and that was good, as I didn't really feel like talking to anyone.

Charlie did come over at one point though just to pass the time of day, but he was the only person I really spoke with.

It seemed very quiet too for a Friday night, but I certainly wasn't complaining.

I just kept thinking about what had happened as I slowly ate my meal.

I kept replaying it over and over in my mind...the height of the thing, how incredibly dark and forceful it felt as it 'looked' down on me, and how it seemed to incredibly engulf my mind completely in an instant! I really did feel like it was going to crush me. Its overwhelming power was so real, so horrendously immense.

My god, that was so scary.

I felt myself just staring across the pub, but looking at nothing as I tried to digest exactly what had taken place.

I found my food an easier task...

I stayed in the Tuns until around 10:00 p.m., and then I made my way back.

I started to think about the cooking or the lack of it, and what I was going to say to Eileen. It was going to be a bit of a tall excuse (if you'll pardon the pun), but I knew she would understand.

And I'll tell you something...I was absolutely dreading going back up to the flat again!

I opened the side door by the practice, pushed the light plunger in and walked down the corridor. I just made it to the concrete stairs; and of course, the light went out...rubbish thing!

I climbed the few stairs, pressed the second light plunger, then entered the walkway and rapped on Jackie's door...but there was no reply.

I unlocked my door... "Once more into the breach..."

I turned on the light and walked slowly up the stairs.

"Have you been having a good time without me?" I said rather anxiously as I walked onto the living-room floor. I could feel the same old muffled heavy atmosphere as I switched on the nearby light switches; my eyes were looking everywhere.

I switched on the kitchen light too and walked slowly down the corridor. The floor seemed to dip more than usual under my footsteps, and the creaking appeared louder than ever...but it was probably the same; in fact, it was the same. It was just my mind exaggerating everything.

I focused directly ahead into the kitchen as I walked; the fluorescent tube trying desperately once more to throw light on the subject.

I looked down at the mince that was sitting there, looking all dejected in the frying pan; and then at the chopped onions and the carrots, that were still waiting patiently to be added into the mix.

Well, it almost happened. My cooking skills would just have to be tested another night.

I picked up the spoon from the sink. The handle felt rough where it had been burnt on the cooker ring, and I picked at it with my thumb nail to remove a few bits of plastic that had bobbled up. I then used the spoon to scrape the beef, onions and carrots into a plastic supermarket bag and then took it downstairs to the dustbin that was just outside the hallway. What a waste! ...but it couldn't be helped.

I came back up, cleaned the work surfaces, put things away and then removed Eileen's instructions from the cupboard door.

I still felt uneasy as I filled the kettle to make some coffee.

I turned to look at the spot again where the black figure had been, and I raised my eyes and looked up as if to gauge its height once more...goodness me; that was horrible, absolutely nightmarish.

I poured out my coffee, and I walked back into the living room.

60

I could feel my nervousness getting stronger. A real feeling of apprehension filled my mind. What was going to happen next, for goodness' sake?

I sat down on the sofa and sipped my coffee.

I really couldn't settle; I was constantly looking around.

Well, so much for me feeling my normal self again!

I sat there for about five minutes, listening to the music, and then I decided to have a quick bath before bed.

My baths were never normally quick, but they certainly were now!

I always loved a good long soak, listening and singing along to music. It was ME time where I could just relax...but unfortunately, not anymore.

Even brushing my teeth and shaving was done at a rate of knots. I just had to get back out into the open space of the living room.

I turned on the bath taps, and it was immediately obvious that the hot water was still *incredibly* hot, absolutely scalding again. I suppose this was all to do with this wretched thing as well! It's all crazy, absolutely crazy!

I went over to the airing cupboard and checked the switch again. I knew damn well it was off, but I just had to see it again with my own eyes. The tank felt absolutely boiling again.

I was in and out of the bath in minutes!

I got into bed and leaned over and turned on the radio.

I lay there listening to Mike Allen on Capital Radio. My mind was buzzing; the radio was really just a background noise as I couldn't stop thinking about the tall black figure, and how I had reacted to its overwhelming appearance...then, I suddenly tuned into what the DJ was saying as he started talking about how he thought his studio was haunted...

Saturday, June 21st
All Happening Above

Incredibly I slept right through to the alarm again, and I certainly must have turned the radio off at some stage in the early hours, but I don't remember doing it.

I was reliving last night's events in my mind as I leaned against the kitchen sink, eating a slice of toast and marmalade…thoughts so vivid, so real; like a film extract on a continuous loop, repeatedly performing like a Chinese water torture. Boy oh boy, I don't think I've never been so scared in all my life.

I washed my hands in the kitchen sink and got ready to go downstairs.

Although I was feeling quite tense, everything else seemed strangely OK in the flat. Thank goodness for that too, because I was almost expecting something odd or strange to be happening all the time now.

I bid the flat a good day and then made my way down to the practice just after 8:30 a.m.

Eileen was in early as well and greeted me with a big smile as she pointed to a waiting mug of tea that was sitting there on the desk.

"Well?" she said, and I knew that was my green light for a tale of culinary expertise…hmm!

I looked at her rather uncomfortably, and then I began the saga of last night's nerve-racking account.

After I had probably bored her with my many animated repeat tellings of the tall black figure, she carefully looked at me straight in the eyes and slowly and calmly said…

"…OK…but…DID YOU COOK THE COTTAGE PIE?"

The morning went by rather quickly as it always seemed to do so on a Saturday; and before we knew it, it was 12:30

p.m....and with everything tidied up and the front door locked, we made our way out to the back office to get ready to leave.

Eileen reminded me again for the umpteenth time to make sure that I would inform Carla of what was happening in the flat, especially now after this latest episode.

She kept asking me if I was alright. I knew that she was concerned about me, but I felt fine...well...sort of fine. This last experience most certainly had been the worst, and it had made me deliberate more on the situation that I was in...but I think I was OK. It didn't interfere with my professional work as a dispensing optician anyway.

I had a sign above the back room doorway leading into the practice that said, "Smile, you're going on stage..." and I firmly believed that. I would don my work mask and would be what Joe public wanted me to be. They certainly didn't come into the practice to hear any of my tales of woe. They were here for me to help them, and that's how I've always worked all my life.

To be honest though, with friends it would only be a small percentage of my persona that I would suppress anyway. I'm really a 'what you see is what you get' sort of chap...but I know Eileen is quite perceptive in the emotional stakes, and I guess it was that small percentage that she was picking up on. Mind you, I think if I was telling you all the things that I was telling Eileen, you might also sit up and be a bit concerned...though probably more for my mental stability than anything else!

After saying goodbye to Eileen, I went upstairs to the flat, greeted the place as normal; then I put on some music and got changed out of my formal shirt and trousers and put on some casual weekend wear.

It was always a lovely feeling on Saturday lunchtime, knowing that I had the whole afternoon to myself.

I opened the fridge door and took out some raspberry ripple ice-cream from the freezer compartment.

Mmmm, this was going to be lunch.

I know, I know...but it was a lovely warm afternoon, and I wasn't very hungry anyway.

I picked up the dessert spoon from the sink and was immediately aware again of the burnt underside of the plastic handle from last night. Why couldn't it have happened to a fork or a knife...I had plenty of those!

I ran it under the tap, wiped it with a tea cloth and then got stuck into the ice-cream as I looked out of the kitchen window and down onto the road below.

The town was really busy. There were lots of people bustling along the pavements.

The sunny warmth of the day was certainly bringing everyone out in their summer clothes. It always felt more like a seaside holiday resort when it was like this. The town certainly had a special atmosphere all to itself.

I stood there doing a bit of people watching for a while, and then I got myself ready to go out.

I'd decided to go for a walk over to the park and to check on my car on the way to make sure that it was actually still there in the residents parking bay…and in one piece!

I only made use of it at weekends; and sometimes, I wouldn't see it for days.

It was a Mitsubishi Colt Celeste which I called Mary. I literally purchased her as I was walking past a car lot in a nearby town. She was sitting there on the forecourt, with two employees adding decals and sprucing her up. She looked superb, and I just went in and bought her, without even a test drive OR even enquiring as to how many miles she'd done. I just liked the look of her, and that was it!

Before Mary, I had a Cortina Mark 4 Sports saloon, which was really lovely, but it attracted the thieves and joy riders; and unfortunately, was broken into twice and stolen THREE times! Hence my concern with Mary now, although she isn't in the same thieving appeal league as the Cortina Sports…thank goodness.

After the second time it was stolen, I decided to sell it, and Eileen's son had shown interest and had met us at the practice after work on a Saturday afternoon for a viewing…and I can see the three of us now in my mind's eye, walking over to the parking area by the church, with Eileen's son expressing his excitement in his eagerness to see it…and then my developing horror when I slowly realised as we got closer to the church that the car wasn't there!

I can still see Eileen's face now as she looked at me with one of her knowing smiles, telling me to stop playing the fool. It took quite a few minutes of apologetic behaviour on my part before she finally accepted that I was being serious.

It was found later the following week, all burnt out in an open car park in a close-by town; and I can remember the expression on the policeman's face, who came to the practice to tell me, when he said, "You can go and have a look at it if you like, but it's not a pretty sight."

I didn't go.

Thankfully, Mary WAS still there, and untouched, and I continued my walk over to the park.

On a Saturday or a Sunday, I liked to go for a long walk around the various parks and the nearby towns and then slowly meander back.

What a day! It was so warm and sunny...absolutely beautiful.

With a bit of luck, we should be able to sit outside the pub tonight and have our drinks on the grass across the road.

I got back to the flat just after 5:00 p.m. and met Jackie returning from the health food store.

I mentioned that I was meeting John and Chris up the pub later, and she insisted we all came around afterwards for a late supper.

I knew what that would involve and that sounded great. The evening was sorted!

I was in the pub around 8 o'clock, and it wasn't long afterwards when Johnny and Chris came bowling in... Well, Chris bowled in...Johnny glided...

We got some drinks, and we did indeed take them outside and sit on the grass along with many other people who had had the same idea.

It was on my mind to tell them both about the flat antics, but John had completely suppressed my thoughts on the matter when he eagerly began telling me of a 'blind' company car auction that was being held at his place of work on Wednesday. He said that he 'knew' of only two other people who were actually interested in participating, and he wanted to know whether it might be something that would appeal to me as well.

A blind auction is where people place sealed bids in envelopes for something, in this case a car; and when the envelopes are opened, the highest bidder would win.

It was for a red Rover 2000 hatchback that was a two-year-old reps car. It had done an average amount of mileage, and it had been serviced regularly by the company; and apparently, it looked as good as new!

I suppose it did sound a bit of an 'old man's' car, but John reckoned that I should be able to get it for around £500! Blimey! …for a two-year-old car!

He said that he'd found out that one of the interested parties was actually going to put in a bid for £500, and that he was fairly sure that the other contender would probably put in a very low and silly bid…so he felt that if I put in a bid for just over £500 to beat the main rival, it would be mine!

Well, it DID appeal to me; especially as Johnny was talking the talk, and he convinced me that it was a done deal. I didn't need a car as I had Mary, but the thought of getting the car for such a cheap price really attracted me, even if it was for just the sell on profit that I could make.

Poor old Chris; I think he just sat there making out he was interested as I talked to John constantly about the auction…

I had already told them both that we'd been invited up to Jackie's later on, and I'm sure that was probably what kept Chris going.

As for any flat business, well…that was a mere speck on the horizon…at the moment!

We got to Jackie's just after 11:15 p.m.

Dolly and Christine had already arrived, and they were both the worst for drink.

Dolly was most definitely one of the moon and stars brigade. She was in her late 30s, around 5'4", full in figure with mauve-coloured long scraggly hair and a stardust face. She would always wear low-cut dresses or tops that would push out her heaving breasts to the point of bursting!

She always came across as very naïve and innocent, but I knew I was most likely the only lad in the town that she hadn't notched onto her bedstead.

Christine was the complete opposite. She was tall with long well-kept blonde hair, fairly quiet and wore clothes to match, but she had a laugh that sounded like it would be more at home coming from Dolly!

John, Chris and I were starving, and good old Jackie had been waiting for us to arrive before serving her famous baked potatoes, and she had cooked us some burgers too…veggie ones, of course!

Her burgers really tasted amazing too. I always wished I'd asked her exactly what she put in them as well, as I've never tasted anything so good in something so simple to this day. Mind you, like I said before…perhaps it was good that I didn't know.

We all sat on the floor and started eating.

Dolly soon took centre stage with stories of the latest man she had been 'fighting off'; and before long the banter was flying, with John, Chris and I taking the mickey out of her misplaced, self-projected, honest-to-goodness innocent behaviour.

We'd been sitting there for about half an hour, talking and laughing, when Christine suddenly sat up straight and put her finger to her mouth, indicating she wanted everyone to be quiet…

"Shssh…listen! What's that?"

Dolly carried on talking, and Christine said it again only much more urgently and directed it at Dolly as she gesticulated to the ceiling…

"No, be quiet…listen!" …and she looked up with wide staring eyes.

Jackie's soft playing background music was rapidly turned off as we all fell completely silent due to the rather desperate, out-of-character behaviour of Christine.

There was a long, silent pause as we all looked at her, then up to the ceiling and then back at Christine again…and I suddenly started to realise that it might be something to do with my flat…

Then…

'CREAK, CREAK, CREAK, CREAK'…came eerily from above.

Oh my goddd! …the hair on my arm stood up as John looked at me and shouted, "Shit, there's someone in your flat!"

Chris jumped up and ran to Jackie's door as I shouted, "No, don't Chris don't, stay here!

…stay here, listen… QUIET! QUIET!"

Everyone was understandably now looking at ME as Johnny had got to his feet too and was at the door with Chris.

"Bloody hell, Steve; let's get up there!"

"No Johnny, hold on, wait, please wait…listen…"

…then Jackie said calmly…

"It's Steve's ghost…"

Dolly screamed, and Chris shouted out a barrage of swear words.

"It's OK…it's OK," I said, with the reassuring tones of a man about to be thrown into the lion pit.

"It's OK…don't worry…sit down… PLEASE!"

Chris was now making up for his lack of talking in the pub and was questioning me like crazy!

All was now quiet from above…and I was just staring at the ceiling…

"STEVE!" said Chris, coming back at me again… "What the bloody hell is going on?"

"I'll go and get some more drinks whilst you tell them," said Jackie, incredibly calmly again, as she threw me a reassuring glance and then got up and walked into the kitchen in her typically unruffled style!

Well…it was like I'd been suddenly asked to take the stand! I had four faces now ardently looking at me. My heart was beating at a rate of knots as I looked at Christine and Dolly. I could see in their eyes that they were scared; their expressions full of uncertainty and apprehension. I was feeling uneasy too, but I was so glad that they had all heard it. It was a real sobering experience for me as well as for them.

I began telling the story, and they all surprisingly just sat quietly and listened as I babbled my way through the account, only being apologetically interrupted by Jackie as she passed out more beers to everyone. Johnny and Chris started to fire questions at me when I'd finished. They both couldn't understand why I hadn't told them earlier…and then Johnny said it…

"It's your bloody loft…I reckon we let the thing out!"

The girls looked at me with puzzled, questionable expressions as I started to recount last Friday's merriment of building the tower upstairs and opening the loft hatch.

I could see John's facial expression starting to change as he digested what I was saying; probably reliving it all in his mind. He then looked at me quite earnestly and convincingly said, "Do you know what…I reckon we DID let it out you know. Do you remember that rush of air that came down? It was cold air, wasn't it? Surely the loft would've been warm at that time of night. It's June! It's summer, for god's sake!"

It was my turn to digest…

The weather had been superb so far this month, and the temperature in the loft would've certainly been fairly warm. The heat from the day would have been quite well-retained up there. It definitely wouldn't have dropped to the temperature of the air that we encountered… Johnny was right!

He then went on to say that he was pretty sure that there had been a fair delay from when I had opened the loft hatch to when the three of us actually experienced the cold air that came rushing down! "I'm certain we were all talking with the hatch open BEFORE we felt that blast of air, you know…"

He looked at me with such conviction in his eyes, awaiting my response.

I sat there staring at Johnny as I absorbed his latest theory.

Everyone had been listening rather intently to what Johnny was saying and were now awaiting my reaction to his latest comment.

I felt my body twitch as I sat there in silence when the realisation of what Johnny had said rang true.

There WAS a delay… I remember. They had asked me what I could see when I stuck my head through the hatch and THEN the air rushed down!

Oh god, this is all too much to take in.

"Are you alright, Steve?" Christine asked me. I think she could see my mind was working overtime, and it certainly was. I was remembering the feeling of the air hugging my body, and I shuddered at the thought of it again as I told them.

Chris stood up at this; his mouth agape, with his arms outstretched in a manner of sudden realisation, as he looked at me and then at Johnny…

"We did let the bugger out!" he said, in a strong conclusive tone.

"Oh bloody hell…" said Dolly, and she shook her head quickly from side to side; her face expressing a look of complete unease and trepidation.

This was horrible. It was suddenly becoming all too factual and tangible now.

I must admit, I had tentatively considered last Friday's escapade as a possible reason for the beginning of all the strangeness, but now taking into consideration all of John's speculations; it certainly seemed a very realistic concept.

Had something really escaped from the attic, and was it now actually living in my flat?

My god, it's all too crazy to comprehend, but John and Chris were very convinced; and to be honest… I was too.

We had all sobered up rather quickly after the creaking from upstairs and the stories. We were still drinking, but we were all remaining quite level-headed and thoughtful.

After I had reacted to John's propositions, I hardly said a thing. I just sat there listening as the theories began to get more and more exaggerated from the 'boys'.

Johnny suggested that the cold air was actually the ghost itself leaving the attic, and that the pressing against my body experience was the spirit itself connecting with me, in order to use me as a host in this world!

Dolly told Johnny to shut up in no uncertain terms, in reaction to that latest pronouncement; and I nervously laughed it off…but I must be honest that the concept scarily stuck with me!

Dolly was relatively quiet though, that night. She just drank her weird-smelling tea, seemingly sipping it forever as she pulled uncomfortable faces in reaction to some of the conversation.

Christine just sat there listening too, but occasionally asked me the odd question, with a very concerned expression…and Jackie…well, Jackie was just being Jackie.

I reckon a bomb could've gone off, and she would've still asked who would like another beer!

It was around 3:00 a.m. when Johnny and Chris decided to go home.

"Come on, Dolly," said John, "We'll walk you back…" and then he looked at me and said, "I'll be in touch; probably Wednesday night…with the good news."

I had to think for a minute, and then I replied, "Oh yeah, thanks John…fingers crossed."…as I realised he was talking about the car auction.

Dolly was listening as she checked through her bag for her flat key and then came over to me and raising her eyebrows said, "That sounds interesting, Steve,"…then added as she leant forward to give me a kiss… "Best of luck with Mr Scary."

I laughed, and we had a hug, then the three of them left.

Christine was staying the night, and Jackie asked whether I wanted to as well.

I think she may've asked it in kindness, not thinking that I would say yes!

…but I didn't need to be asked twice…there was NO WAY I was going back upstairs at this time of night, especially after what had happened, and what with all the stuff we had been discussing still fresh in my mind. Blimey, I think I would've slept downstairs in the practice if she hadn't of suggested anything.

I could hear Christine and Jackie softly talking in the bedroom as I lay on the living room floor under a blanket, with my hands behind my head, staring up into the space that was the ceiling. It was being very quietly illuminated from the street lamp across the road as my eyes tried to follow every line and contour in its aging pattern.

I was wide awake, reflecting on all that had happened tonight, whilst straining my ears to hear any sound, any cracking or creaking that might emanate from upstairs…ridiculously imagining this thing prowling around, waiting for me to return.

NO CHANCE! …not tonight anyway…

Sunday, June 22nd
Lazy Sunday Afternoon

I put my head around Jackie's bedroom door around 10:30 a.m. and thanked her for letting me stay. She got up and came over and gave me a hug, and we both smiled at each other as Christine made a loud snorting snoring sound.

She quietly opened her front door to let me out and then waited for me to open mine. She then gave me a knowing and understanding wave and went back inside.

I was craning my neck as I walked up the stairs and into the flat.

I was more on edge than I had ever been…if that was possible.

I walked out onto the living room floor which was bathed in warm sunlight, and I looked around the room.

Everything seemed OK, but I could feel the close oppressive atmosphere once more.

Boy oh boy, I really hated it now.

I carried on down to the kitchen, having a look into the bathroom on the way, and again everything seemed as it should be. I never knew what I was looking for when I did my glancing around the flat. It was just reassuring myself that everything was in its right place and had not been moved I guess.

"Good!" I said out loud, "and a GOOD morning to you, Mr Scary!" I added even louder as I went into the bathroom to run a bath.

The water came out as usual piping hot, and again I went to the immersion cupboard to feel the tank and to look at that switch! Yep, it was still definitely in the off position, and I knew it would be, but I just had to look. I didn't really have to feel the tank either because of the heat that hit me as soon as I opened the cupboard door.

I had a very quick bath with the door wide open once more. My awareness of the corridor outside and my fraying nerves rather speeding the process again.

I then made some toast, had a cup of tea, and then put on some shorts and a t-shirt and got ready to go out.

I had arranged with a lady called Mrs Ziegler, a patient of the practice, to take her dog out over the park for a walk later this morning as she had to go into the city quite early; and there was no way her elderly mother (who lived with her) could do it.

The dog in question was the biggest Irish wolfhound you ever did see called Barney, and they lived a few streets away in the town.

I had got to know Barney quite well as I would often see them both in the park and would regularly stop to have a chat (with Mrs Zeigler!), and it was a couple of weeks ago when she mentioned the early morning trip, and I offered to help.

It was about 11:30 a.m. when I knocked on her door, and Barney sauntered out with a ball in his mouth as Mrs Zeigler's mother looked on.

It was another warm summer's day, with the sun shining down from an almost cloudless blue sky, as we walked over towards the park area.

I had been looking forward to walking Barney. I would've gone for a walk anyway, as I felt really heady after last night and needed the fresh air, but this was better being with him. He almost felt like he was my dog as we walked side by side across the grass.

I'd throw his ball, and he would lollop after it. He'd then pick it up in his mouth, turn, and then run back full pelt at me, swerving at the last moment to avoid collision. Now, Mrs Ziegler had told me he'd do this, and she advised me to just stand still; otherwise I'd get bowled over!

I could see it in his eyes that he loved doing it, but after about the fourth run of watching this mammoth of a dog coming at me, I lost faith in his ability to avoid me...so the ball stayed in my hand for the rest of the walk, though Barney did his utmost to get me to change my mind!

We got back to Mrs Ziegler's around 1:00 p.m. Barney was panting like mad and needed a drink and a lay down, and I needed a drink and something to eat!

I made my way back to the practice and opened the side door and started walking up to the flat.

As I rounded the concrete stairs, I came across Dolly and Christine sunbathing on the flat roof, just before the hallway.

I immediately smiled as I saw that Dolly was topless (what a surprise), and I could see that she was observing my line of sight, so I made absolutely sure that I concentrated on her face.

Jackie was emerging from her flat with some drinks and asked me if I wanted to join them.

It was tempting, but I was hungry, and I'd already made my mind up that I was going next door to the wine bar; so I declined, and unlocked my door and went upstairs to the flat.

As soon as I walked out onto the living-room floor, I noticed my plate with toast crumbs from earlier, that was sitting on the floor by the orange armchair…and YES, that's where I had left it too! Good!

I asked Mr Scary if he had missed me as I walked through into the bedroom to change my shorts for some trousers.

The talking to the flat, and now referring to the other occupier as Mr Scary (thank you Dolly), was just part and parcel now; and every time I did it, I would also be looking around, like I was playing some kind of hide-and-seek game with him.

I guess I did it to try to be friendly to the thing too, but I know it was just my nerves…and I cannot impress on you strongly enough how incredibly nervous and tense I was most of the time when I was in the flat.

It was a constant 'on edge' feeling, thinking I was sharing my flat with this unknown entity that seemed like it was going to do something to scare me all the flamin' time!

I just knew somehow though, in a strange sort of way, that it wasn't actually going to do anything to ME…that it wasn't going to really harm me in any way.

I cannot explain that feeling.

Perhaps it was just me trying to convince myself that it didn't mean me any harm, I don't know.

I went back down stairs; passing Dolly's exposed body on the way and made my way around to the wine bar. A jacket potato with melted cheese and prawns, washed down with a glass of wine, was my favourite, mmm lovely…and that was the order of today too.

It was more of an up-market eating establishment in the town (the only reason I changed out of my shorts), frequented by lots of well-heeled people; even a few well-known celebrities sometimes, but none today…well, none that I can see anyway.

Mind you, Eileen came over to me all excited in the practice the other day and said as she pointed across the practice with her eyes, "Have you seen who's sitting in the waiting room?"

Apparently it was some 'famous' actor who was playing up the West End at the time, but I didn't recognise him, and I certainly hadn't heard of him.

So for all I know, I'm probably surrounded by famous actors today!

The wine bar had a downstairs entertaining area too, which was like a cave, with little alcoves and small tables for private cosy get-togethers; but I was upstairs on my own, sitting by the window, watching the world go by.

I started to think again about Mr Scary.

I certainly wouldn't ever call OUR get-togethers cosy!

It's amazing how something or someone can so easily take over your thoughts sometimes to the point where it seems that all you can ever think about is them! I was actually looking forward to going back to work tomorrow to try and get Mr Scary out of my head so to speak. Dealing with our demanding patients and the general concentration needed to ensure that I met their needs would certainly occupy my main thoughts. But I was also looking forward to seeing Carla again and telling her about my new flat mate too, so I guess he wouldn't be out of my mind for long.

Eileen had certainly given me the impression that Carla could help me in some mysterious way. Goodness knows how though…but it was very intriguing.

I finished my lunch and headed back to the flat.

Christine and Jackie were sitting on the steps drinking, as I walked through, and Dolly was still lying on a sponge sun mat…keeping abreast of things!

I sat down on a higher step behind them, and we started chatting.

Dolly sat up and asked me if anything else had happened in the flat since last night. She added that the creaky floor experience and all the talk that had transpired had scared her absolutely silly. I said that I had noticed that she had been rather quiet, which made her smile. She went on to say that she hadn't slept much either because she just kept thinking about it all the time.

Poor Dolly; she certainly looked upset as she told me all this. It really had got to her.

Christine tried to make light of it all by saying, "Well, think of Steve, he's living with the thing!"

Sunday night passed without any incident.

I spent most of the evening lying on the sofa, listening to dance tapes, drinking milk and snacking on peanuts.

I loved evenings like this, with the music playing, eating and relaxing...but I do use the word 'relaxing' rather loosely. I constantly kept looking around the flat, especially towards the stairwell; but thankfully, all remained fine.

In fact, this was the best evening I'd had for quite a while in the flat. It was almost like how it used to be before Mr Scary had come to stay.

I went to bed around midnight and fell asleep listening to Capital Radio.

Monday, June 23rd
Heavy Stuff

I opened my eyes and leaned closer to the clock to see the time.

It had just gone 3:00 a.m. again!

I turned off the radio and lay there, staring up at the dark ceiling.

Everything was quiet…and I must have soon nodded off again.

BUZZ! BUZZ! BUZZ! BUZZ!

I didn't beat the alarm this time. I went straight into the bathroom, cleaned my teeth and had a shave.

It was toast for breakfast again, with a cup of tea. I never really could eat much first thing, but always by around 10:00 a.m., I could've eaten for England!

I went down to the practice around 8:40 a.m. and did my normal work preparation.

I had just put Carla's coffee on the desk in the back office when in she walked.

Her skin was always fairly well-tanned, but today it was even more so; and she was wearing a yellow, slightly off-the-shoulder dress to show it all off.

"Did you miss me then?" she said with a cheeky grin as she went straight to the long mirror and started to adjust her waistband.

I liked working with Carla; she made the day a fun day…and I had missed her.

We had no sight testing going on, but we were fairly steady all morning, with people coming and going.

Carla told me some holiday stories and said that she would show me some funny photos, when she got around to getting them developed.

I told her that I had some stories to tell her too; and in between seeing patients, I gave her an overview of what had been going on upstairs in the flat.

She was very interested indeed and said that if I didn't object, she'd like to go up to the flat at lunch time to take a look around. The expression on her face became quite thoughtful and serious as she went on to say that she'd always felt that she could sense the supernatural, and she added that her mother had the 'gift' too.

Well…that was it then. I understood why Eileen wanted me to tell Carla now. It looks like she was a bit of a ghost buster after all!

She suddenly became this pensive fountain of knowledge on ghosts and spirits, and the conversations that morning became wrapped around her experiences of when she was a child, and her understandings of the paranormal.

Blimey! This was the side of Carla I certainly hadn't seen before!

As soon as we closed for lunch, she wanted to go up to the flat; and before long, I had opened my front door, and we were walking up the stairs.

Under normal circumstances, she would have been joking about coming up here with me, making lots of innuendos…but not today.

I stopped at the top of the stairs and let her walk through onto the living room floor, where she stood still and took a deep breath.

I could sense the same old, normal, strange, closed-in feeling straight away, and I asked her if she could sense it too, but she said that she could not.

I was so sure she'd say yes as well.

"Do you mind if I wander around?" she asked as she looked back at me.

I just held my hands out in a sort of 'please, help yourself' manner, and off she went…

She walked around the living room, then into my bedroom…and then down to the kitchen.

I stood in the living room, watching her, as the floor creaked below her careful footsteps.

She paused and turned to walk back. She had a frown on her face, her lips pushed forward into a pout giving a thoughtful expression as she looked at me and slowly shook her head from side to side as if to say 'nothing here'.

Then she stopped at the entrance to the bathroom and walked inside…

It was then, after about five seconds, that all hell broke loose, as she practically ran out with a look of horror on her face and stormed past me and headed for the stairs.

"It's in the bathroom! It's in the bathroom!" she said in a very strong, panic-stricken voice; her eyes wide and staring as I chased after her down the stairs.

"Carla! Carla!"

I followed her all the way down to the side entrance of the practice, where she stopped and turned to face me.

"Stop it, Carla; you're scaring me…what did you see?"

"I'm sorry, Steve, it's in your bathroom. I didn't see it…but I know it's in there!"

I quickly opened the practice side door and immediately pulled out one of the chairs and indicated for Carla to make use of it. She was visibly shaking as she sat down and looked at me with another expression on her face that I hadn't seen from her before…it was one of fright!

I felt really all at sea…we were at 'work' in the back office for goodness' sake; but in a situation so alien to anything else I had ever encountered, or would hopefully ever likely to encounter again with a work colleague…and this was Carla…joking, cheeky, saucy Carla…nothing gets to Carla!

I didn't know what to say. I just looked back at her as I sunk down on my knees and instinctively took hold of her quivering hand.

I'm sure it would've looked quite funny to an onlooker with me, kneeling there on the floor, looking up at her, as I gently squeezed her hand in an attempt to reassure her that everything was OK.

I was just going to ask if she was alright when she said…

"Go and make us a cup of tea, you soft sod…go on."

She smiled as she said it…and suddenly she was back. It was the old Carla once more.

I thankfully got up and put the kettle on as she gradually started to tell me what had just happened.

She apologised for running out of my flat but explained that she just had to physically get away because she could feel that it was trying to penetrate her mind.

She didn't see anything, but she had 'heard' and had felt its immense power from high up in the bathroom. She said it was like she was being shouted at.

When I enquired as to what it had said she replied that it was not really words, but more like a rush of sounds in the head that she likened to shouting.

I started to question her as Chris did to me in Jackie's flat, but I could see that she wasn't handling it very well and so I stopped.

After we closed the practice later and were about to leave, Carla came up to me and said that she didn't know how I was putting up with it all, but assured me that she didn't think it was going to do me any harm.

"It won't be there for long, Steve, so don't worry," she added as she picked up her bag to go out the side door of the practice.

I walked Carla down the passage way; and as I opened the front door, I said that I was sorry for what had happened today…and I genuinely meant it.

I could tell it had really affected her as she had been very quiet during the afternoon.

She told me again not to be so soft, but admitted that she had been thinking about it a lot, though she wanted to reiterate that she felt it wasn't going to stay long.

I hoped that she was right.

I closed the door and walked back to the practice. I didn't quite feel like going back up to the flat yet, so I went back into the office and put the kettle on for some more tea.

I stood there leaning against the sink and thinking.

I wish she'd never said that it was powerful.

Mind you, I knew that it was anyway by what it did to me in the kitchen…but hearing it from someone else seemed to make it even more powerful if that makes any sense at all?

It was the look on her face and the way she almost pushed past me to get out of the flat earlier, that was disturbing too; and although she apologised and explained her reasons for doing so, it still added to my own concerns.

I also started thinking about when she said, "It wasn't going to do me any harm."

I sort of felt that myself too, but how could she know for sure? Was she just saying that to make me feel easier?

Carla is fairly straight-forward though, quite black and white, so I think she would've told me if she had any real worries.

But I just couldn't get the expression on Carla's face out of my mind, when she brushed past me upstairs in the flat. It was simply one of sheer terror! ...and I had also mentally noted that she had described the powerful presence as being 'up high'.

Oh boy! It was that overpowering height thing again, just like I had in the kitchen.

I stayed in the back office for 20 minutes or so, putting off the inevitable by doing unnecessary tidying whilst finishing off that cup of tea.

I then went up to the flat, unlocked the front door and walked slowly up the stairs.

I got to the top, stopped and looked around.

Everything seemed normal, and I use the word normal rather loosely.

I walked down the corridor towards the kitchen and hovered around the bathroom door and looked in. I automatically looked up to the corners of the room as I turned on the light, but I sensed nothing, and there was certainly nothing to see...and I really knew there wouldn't be anyway.

"Only going to show yourself on your own terms, ay?" I said out loud.

I was feeling nervous as usual, but I had an underlying feeling of annoyance and almost anger again.

This thing was not only affecting me, but it was affecting friends and now my work colleagues too.

"Come on, show yourself...do something!" I said as I walked back onto the living-room floor.

I think if it had of done though, I would've done a Carla...only 100 times quicker!

I got changed out of my work stuff, said goodbye to Mr Scary rather sarcastically, and headed around to the Indian restaurant, buying an *Evening Standard* on the way.

I was starving and was really looking forward to a Chicken Tikka Masala, mmm, with half an Indian lager, of course!

I sat there on my own, reading the paper, looking up once to acknowledge one of the 'Silent Club', who came in shortly after me.

What a lunchtime! ...and poor Carla...I felt really bad with myself for putting her through all that. I certainly would have thought twice about letting her go up into the flat if I'd known things were going to happen in the way that they did.

I left the restaurant around 7:30 p.m. and headed back to the practice.

I decided I'd better phone Carla to see how she was. I really felt quite guilty, and I wanted to make sure she was alright.

I sat down out in the back office and dialled her number. She answered in quite a cheery voice, which made me feel much better immediately.

She was absolutely fine and started apologising again for her actions earlier.

Now that I knew she was in a better state of mind, I began to ask her questions about the incident, and what she felt she saw...well, pictured in her mind.

She described it as similar to my kitchen incident. It was an incredibly tall, dark force that leant over her as she stood in the bathroom. She added that she could feel it staring down at her, trying to push into her mind and reinforced again that that was the reason why she just had to get away rather rapidly.

I asked her how she could possibly really know that it wasn't going to harm me...I had to ask.

Carla said that although it scared her initially, she could feel afterwards that it had an impish, almost mischievous nature; and that it was this that gave her the impression that it didn't mean me any harm. I compared it to the spoon on the floor, and the sofa being moved that I had accounted to her earlier.

"Exactly," she said, "it comes over as harum-scarum like and not malicious."

"It certainly knows how to scare 'em, alright," I quipped...and Carla laughed.

"He does like to scare," she said in a monotone, jokey-type voice.

"…but there's one other thing too, and this is the other reason I feel he will not harm you. I can sense that he cares for you," she continued. "I know that sounds absolutely ridiculous, but I think I can feel it."

Now that did make me laugh. A ghost that likes to scare me; but at the same time, is worried about my well-being? Crazy!

We must have carried on talking about it all for close on to an hour!

"Do you know what, we should've stayed at work!" she said.

"Yes, and at this rate, it'll be time to GO back to work too!" I laughingly added.

We finished the call, joking with each other, as we said goodnight.

It was great to finish the phone call like that too. It was back to the usual cheeky Carla.

WELL! I now felt so incredibly different in my mind!

I actually felt happier…I could feel myself smiling as I sat there thinking about what she had said.

For the first time in about ten days, I almost felt like my normal happy-go-lucky self…it was a superb feeling! …and I say 'almost' because I was still very wary of Mr Scary. That feeling couldn't just simply disappear in a phone call. But listening to Carla's understanding of him had certainly lightened it all.

Mr Scary is basically a practical joking poltergeist then, with a bit of a kind-hearted nature? That's exaggerating it rather a lot, but it certainly made me feel so much easier thinking of him like that now.

I noticed that Carla referred to it as HIM too. A Mrs Scary would have certainly been so much easier to handle…I think!

I smiled to myself as I thought that, and also about 'a practical joking poltergeist', and my mind wandered as I sat there thinking of a practical joke that I had played on Eileen and Carla earlier during the year.

Excuse me whilst I digress again…I had bought this little joke tape player contraption that was designed to be fitted behind a toilet. It had a plastic tube coming from the device that was attached to a plastic air bulb that fitted under the rim of the seat. The idea being that when someone sat on the seat, their weight would squeeze air from the bulb and down the tube, which would start a tape playing in the unit that said in an American voice, "Hey! ...I'm working down here!"

I'd tried it out myself, and it really made me laugh, more so thinking though how the 'girls' would react when I set them up with it.

So picture this...I'd put it in the toilet, which was situated just outside the side door of the practice by the concrete stairs, on a day when they were both working with me, and I kept watch on them, with the plan being that when one of them went outside to go, I'd run quickly to open the side door slightly to listen, so I could hear the 'scream!' and I would laugh my head off...well, that was the plan anyway.

They must have gone to the toilet a few times during the morning, and each time I was standing by the side door listening...but there was no American voice...and this went on until just before lunchtime where I'd finally had had enough, and I went out there and pressed the seat to see what had gone wrong. Sure enough, on came the voice saying, "Hey! I'm working down here!"...followed by Eileen and Carla laughing THEIR heads off...standing right behind me in the corridor!

It turns out Carla had seen the contraption and had warned Eileen earlier, but the funniest thing about it all was when they told me that it would never have worked with them anyway, as they BOTH never sat down on public toilet seats!

WELL! ...I couldn't believe it! ...and this really amused me as my mind worked overtime, visualising them, amazingly trying to hover over the seat, and I kept joking and going on about it with them for the rest of the afternoon.

It still makes me smile today...in fact, so much so that I've just phoned Eileen to see how she's doing, and I've just asked her if she remembered the toilet seat joke. "Of course I do!" she said, and she added that she tells people that those times with me and Carla were the happiest of her working days.

That feels so good.

Anyway...back to Mrs Scary...sorry, I mean MR Scary.

I went back up to the flat, opened the door and walked up the stairs to the top, and then strode across the floor with purposeful strides down to the kitchen to get a lager out of the fridge.

As I said, I was feeling quite differently mentally, much more at ease.

I came back through to the living room, switched on the disco unit tape player and turned the volume up.

YES! …this was more like it.

I started jigging around the living room, doing my best Michael Jackson moves with a can of lager in my hand.

Isn't it amazing how a few words from someone can totally change your whole persona?

This was me now…I felt more relaxed, and it felt so good.

I soon finished the can and was returning to the fridge for another.

"Come on then, Scary Boy, let me see you do your stuff! Do you fancy a dance? Let's see what you can do!" I shouted out as I pulled the ring on the second can.

I was dancing from room to room, 'looking' for Mr Scary.

It was antagonising talk; perhaps I could push him over his spiritual edge with my provoking…not that I had an agenda here…it just came out that way. I was exasperated with it all really, and I think the suppressed emotions of anger and frustration were coming through.

I was looking up into the corner of the rooms, telling him to come down and join me…daring him to come and play!

I was in control, and boy did I feel it.

I know it was the drink, but I just didn't feel at all bothered as I strutted around the flat, spouting out obscenities and telling him what a pain he'd been since he'd moved in. Garbled sentences of criticism were flying from my mouth as I wandered around pointing and gesticulating.

Mind you, if he was in the living room, he would have to be a lip reader as the music was drowning out my rantings; but he would've got the general gist of things from my body language and my facial expressions.

You're probably thinking to yourself I'd gone on off my rocker, but it was honestly pure exasperation and retaliation for the last ten days or so…and as I said, I know the drink was fuelling it all, but it relaxed my mind enough to allow my strength of feeling to really come to fruition.

"I'll give him harum-scarum alright! He likes to frighten does he? Bloody soddin' thing!"

My rather confrontational behaviour gradually subsided as I succumbed to the realisation that he wasn't going to respond.

I was already on my third lager, and this for me was probably a bit too much for a Monday night anyway… a bit too much for me ANY NIGHT really!

I could quite easily get merry on one, let alone three (not forgetting the Indian half, of course), and I could feel my body requiring the stabilising, sitting-down assistance of the sofa.

I put my can of lager on the table, reduced the music volume, then plonked myself down on the settee with legs akimbo and sat there in a slight haze, just staring into space. I felt good, totally relaxed, and I slowly closed my eyes and let my head slump back on the sofa and after a while I dozed off…

I awoke with a start as the tape player automatically switched off with a BANG!

Damn thing!…it had done that to me so many times when I'd been dozing…and I really do mean a BANG…it would make you jump even if you weren't half-asleep.

I relaxed back again on the sofa. It was almost dark outside, and I sat there with my head leaning back, looking at the ceiling.

I started to doze off again…

THUD!

Whoa! I sat up with a real start this time, with my eyes wide open, just in time to see my can of lager falling from the table and spurting a big splash of drink onto the carpet as it hit the floor in front of me.

I jumped up and picked up the can to prevent more lager coming out.

How the ruddy hell did that happen? Did the table move? Was that the thud? It had felt like the whole floor had shaken.

Let's get some more lights on.

I switched on the main living-room light and went back over to the table.

It did look like it was in a slightly different position.

I moved closer…

There was a heavy, dark-green patterned, rug-type cloth that was draped over it, that hung down low on all four sides. It had been there since I'd moved in. It had a soft felt like feel in certain parts of the pattern, and I always thought it was something that the Victorians would have had draped over their tables.

I got down on my knees and lifted the cloth to see the table centre base, and straight away I could see the indentation in the carpet where it had been sitting for years…was now to one side!

Oh my god! The table HAD moved…was that Mr Scary's doing? …of course, it was!

…and blimey…that table weighs an absolute ton!

I sat back down on the sofa.

He's gone and done it again, hasn't he.

…he's waited until I was all calm, quiet and relaxed…and then attacked!

I sat there, just staring at the table. *Go on; do it again,* I thought.

I was rooted to the spot, just turning things over in my mind…did he tip the table? …did he lift it? …he must have lifted it straight up a bit and dropped it back down to make the thud sound, otherwise it would've just rocked on the centre if he'd tipped it! My head and body twitched as I imagined it happening right in front of my eyes…well, my closed eyes anyway. I so wished I'd seen it, and then I'd know he'd done it. Mind you…seeing it actually happening might've been too much to take in if you know what I mean. I'd not seen anything really happen…it was all after the event or in my mind so to speak…and I think that's how I was managing it all really. To see a table lifting up and come thumping down in front of me would most likely have finished me off!

I finally got up and looked over at my alarm clock in the bedroom…just gone 10:30 p.m.…I need a coffee.

I went down to the kitchen and put on the kettle.

The booze was still affecting me, but I felt OK as I put an extra sugar in my mug. Sweet coffee always seemed to straighten my head after a bit of 'drink'…and it certainly needed straightening after this latest Mr Scary episode.

I kept thinking of the immense force needed to shift that table as I stood there making my cuppa. But I also kept reminding myself of what Carla had said, and what she had implied…that he was simply just playing…and that he just liked to scare.

Well, I'll tell you something…he was doing a flamin' good job!

Tuesday, June 24th
Second Thoughts

I woke up just gone 3:00 a.m. again.

I think my mind was doing this now automatically, similar to how it would normally wake me up just before the alarm went off. I don't think it was anything to do with old Scary pants, though I would still lay there 'listening' to the silence with eyes wide open, until I fell back to sleep.

I did beat the alarm again when I woke up next, had my usual minimum breakfast, and got ready for work.

I felt the water tank when I went around to the bathroom and it was STILL baking hot…and I certainly now DID believe that that was due to him too…it had to be; and to be honest, that didn't bother me at all. Now the table on the other hand…boy oh boy!

I walked over and lifted up the cloth on one side again, only this time lifting it onto the table top itself and looked at the indentation in the carpet. I then grabbed hold of the table from underneath and pulled with all my might to move it back on to its 'spot'.

It shifted back, but my goodness; it took quite an effort of pulling and tugging…it was ridiculously heavy.

I stood there looking at it as I adjusted my tie.

How could he have lifted that; I can barely make the thing move even by pulling it.

Mind you, I was still only assuming that it had been lifted because I couldn't think of any other explanation. I pulled the cloth back down again and carried on getting ready.

I met Carla coming down the side passageway of the practice, just before 8:30 a.m.

"YOU are bright and early," I said in a cheery voice as I unlocked the side door and turned on the lights.

She followed me inside and put her bag on the table as I deactivated the alarm.

I glanced at her face for she hadn't said anything as I started to fill the kettle with water…she looked rather pensive…

"Steve…" and she said it with a tone that reminded me straight away of Eileen…

"I've been thinking about what I said to you last night…and I think that you SHOULD be careful."

Carla had a pretty smiling face, but this morning, it was all stern and serious again.

She went on to say that although she could feel the childlike playful side of the poltergeist, she realised now that she couldn't be 100 percent sure that it didn't have a hidden agenda.

"What do you mean by hidden agenda?" I asked rather quickly…I could feel my body tensing.

Carla looked at me and said, "Sorry Steve, I don't want to get you worried…" and then she explained how some spirits can be devious and put up a soft front, that hides a more sinister side…she went on to say that this probably wasn't the case here, but just to be aware of it…

Oh great! …here we go again!

I told Carla about the moving table incident and that I'd said a few things to possibly provoke him (cough, cough), and she quickly interrupted me and said, in no uncertain terms, that I must NEVER do that again.

"…you REALLY would be stoking up the fire doing that…" she added.

Like I said earlier, it's amazing how a few words or a sentence can change your whole persona…and now, unfortunately, this had knocked me back down again.

I know Carla was right to say how she felt…she was obviously concerned about the situation, and she does clearly seem to have some kind of understanding about all this sort of thing anyway, so far be it for me to doubt anything she said.

I just wish it would all stop, so that I can go back to living my normal life again.

We had a morning clinic running which seemed to fly by.

It was good to see and hear Carla being on great form with the patients, and I could tell she was pampering me more than usual too.

At lunchtime, after the doctor had packed up and gone, we sat out in the back office and chatted whilst eating our sandwiches.

I had a big grin on my face as I asked her whether she wanted to go upstairs to experience the flat again.

Carla stopped from taking another bite of her sandwich and looked at me with her cheeky smile…

"I'm afraid on this occasion, Steve; I think I will just have to say no."

"Oh Carla…" I responded in a very disappointing tone, but still with a big grin on my face.

We spoke more about her holiday, and what she was going to do with her next block of time off which was in August. She asked me whether I'd actually still be here to hear all about it, as she knew I'd been enquiring about a vacancy for a dispensing optician elsewhere.

It was Eileen that had spurred me on with this really. She often said, "Not that I want to see you go Steve, BUT…" And then, she'd come out with the reasons a chap of my age should not be renting property but buying. I understood where she was coming from as my job here also had the flat taken into consideration in my salary. She also reckoned I could be making a lot more money elsewhere, AND be investing in bricks and mortar at the same time.

It was just over four years that I'd been here, and although I was really enjoying it, I knew she was right in what she was saying, so I had been looking…and in fact, there was something in the pipeline that I hadn't told anyone about yet.

"Is it your friend upstairs that's driving you away?" Carla inquired.

"He's not ruddy helping!" I replied.

Mr Scary certainly wasn't helping, but I would've left anyway whether he'd shown up or not; but at the moment, he was definitely not persuading me to stay.

The afternoon was the opposite of the morning. It went really slowly and was very quiet, and we spent most of the time doing general housekeeping, seeing the odd patient (and boy, they certainly can be odd) and talking as we went along.

I made an effort to talk about anything BUT the flat, and I think Carla did the same; and we had quite a fun time in the end, reminiscing and talking of future plans.

I didn't mention to Carla that I'd already been offered a job. I wanted Eileen to be the first to know…and I hadn't actually accepted it yet anyway, although I was pretty sure I was going to.

We finished dead on time, locked the front door and made our way out the back to go 'home'. There was no clearing up to do because we'd done it, and done it, and done it again! …yes, it definitely was one of those afternoons.

Carla asked me what I was going to be doing tonight as she rummaged around in her bag.

It was another lovely, warm, sunny evening again, so I had planned to go for a walk, with a bit of a run here and there.

"What about you?" I enquired.

"Well," she said with a smile, "My walk, and with no running involved I might add, will be the journey home, then they'll be lots of sitting around tonight watching the TV."

She said that she felt tired, and I knew what she meant. It always seemed to drain you more when business was slow.

We said goodbye, and as she left to go she hesitated, then turned around and said, "Do you know what, I see more of you and probably talk to you more than I do to my husband!"

She said it with a thoughtful look on her face, and all I could do in reaction was to laugh.

"It's just an observation, Steve…strange though, isn't it?"

I knew what she meant. When I thought about it (and I did)…it was the same for me too when considering my friends. I saw more of Carla than any of them…and probably Eileen too as well. She didn't work as many days as Carla, but I reckon she was in second spot as to the person I spent the most time with.

I set the alarm, locked the side door and made my way up to the flat.

As I opened the door and walked up the stairs, I could feel that bloody closed-in sensation again. I didn't feel it so much yesterday after I spoke with Carla on the phone. It did make me wonder whether so much of it is my mind control. Yesterday, I was obviously on a high with Carla's talk lessening the seriousness of the situation, and perhaps the mind then isn't so sensitive and open to receiving these kind of feelings…I don't know…anyway, I could definitely sense it now as I went through into the bedroom and got changed into some shorts.

I came back out and put on some music, then went into the bathroom and had a quick splash in the sink to freshen up.

I'd have a soak in the bath tonight if I could control my nerves…get a bit of a disco bath going on. I hadn't had a good soak for ages.

I remember a few months back now, buying a big fat cigar that I proposed to smoke in the bath, because I'd seen it done so many times in films. I'd seen Burt Reynolds and Clint Eastwood do it, and I wanted to see what all the fuss was about.

I remember lying there, trying unsuccessfully to keep the cigar dry as I puffed away with the smoke filling the entire bathroom.

I think I felt like Joe Cool for about 30 seconds, and then the smoke and the soggy cigar became so annoying that I had to get out!

I should add that I don't even smoke! …but it was one of those things that I had to try… ONCE!

I put on a t-shirt and some plimsolls and stood at the top of the stairs and looked over to the dining table, then up to the corner of the room. I was imagining where he'd be right now, and the corner of the room behind the table seemed the obvious place at the moment. I stared high into the corner for a good 20 seconds. I wanted him to appear, I wanted him to make a noise…do something, do anything…but I knew he wouldn't. He would probably be waiting for me in the bathroom for when I get back.

Now, that wasn't such a good thought!

I slowly descended the stairs, still looking into the living-room corners for any signs and then made my way down and out of the building.

It was a lovely, warm, blue-skied, sunny evening, with a scattering of fluffy clouds as I walked up the road and past the crawling traffic that was trying to move down and through the town. I crossed over onto the grass and made my way over to the park, checking on my car by the church, and yes…it was still there!

As I got near the middle of the park, I sat down on the grass, with my hands spread out behind me and took in the view. I often used to do this. The town is such a special place: it really is; and out here, I felt like I was in my own little, simple world, watching the big real complicated world go silently by.

I looked back at the church and the buildings. I could see the stationary caterpillar of metal that was there on the grass horizon. It was going somewhere, but it was really going nowhere.

It seemed like day-to-day life was going on all around me, and I was in the quiet centre, looking out at it all.

What's that old saying? 'Stop the world. I want to get off'? Well, this was always a great place to do just that.

I'd always get quite philosophical when I was out here too, and as I lay back with my hands behind my head, I looked to the huge sky above me and imagined…

When I was living back with my parents, I used to go around the village with a friend one evening, every two weeks, collecting money for a charity…and on one of those evenings, we were sitting chatting on our motorbikes at the bottom of a hill when we spotted a light in the night sky, and we both sat perfectly still, watching it. It had caught our eyes because of its speed…but then, it suddenly slowed and did an incredible side to side motion before speeding up again and continuing across the sky.

Well! No plane could do that, and there was absolutely no sound either.

I remember we both let out a 'WOW!' in amazement, as we rushed to put our helmets back on, started our bikes and sped up the hill to follow it as it carried on its flight path.

We were not fast enough though; and by the time we reached the brow of the hill, it had long gone.

But ever since that experience, I've been totally convinced that there is something going on up there in the skies that cannot always be explained EVERY TIME, with present day technology and natural phenomena.

Could people from another planet be visiting Earth?

Could people from Earth in the future be visiting Earth?

Now I know that sounds a bit far-fetched, unless you're into that sort of thing...but if someone had told me that I was going to experience all the stuff that I've experienced so far in the flat...well, I wouldn't have believed them either!

> *'I look up high to the smoke filled grounds,*
> *Of hills and fields clogged up with sounds,*
> *Where man's creations make their way,*
> *Through past and present to the future day.'*

...on we go...

I had a walk and a jog around, and then I started to make my way back.

I was starting to feel a bit hungry and thought I'd go straight out after getting changed; so no more jogging as I didn't want to be all hot and sweaty.

The traffic was flowing easier through the town now as I walked over to the central shopping area. People were sitting outside the pub on the corner, having drinks, and I started to think where I should go tonight for something to eat.

I'd only ever been in there on a lunch time with Eileen or with a frame rep, who was trying to butter me up...and besides, I always thought that the evenings there were a bit laddish anyway, and I really didn't fancy that tonight.

I went up to the flat, and after having a good look around as normal, I had another quick splash and then got myself changed into my red baggies and a blue thin flowery cotton t-shirt.

I was very aware of the flat atmosphere as usual, but I was moving around quite quickly, and I think I didn't give myself much time to digest too much of it. Perhaps that was the answer, just keep on the go!

I had a last look around, and everything seemed OK and where it should be. I wished Mr Scary a pleasant few hours without me as I grabbed some money and made my way down the stairs.

Jackie's door was wide open, and I leant inside and shouted, "See you in a bit, Jacks!" She immediately came bounding out with a tea towel in her hand as I was walking away.

"Are you dining out again, my Lord?" she inquired, with a smile.

That made me smile too, and I was stuck with a reply for a moment, as Jackie never really normally made funny quips like that.

"See you soon…" I replied in the end, with a confused laugh and a nod of my head, as I skipped down the stairs.

I went around to the Tun's and ordered a chicken and chips in a basket and a pint of Tennant's top, and I sat down with my *Evening Standard.*

Charlie appeared from behind the scenes and gave me a wink of acknowledgement as I was looking around to see who was in…

About a month ago, I was in here with a few friends that had come down to stay.

It was quite a busy Saturday night; and as we sat at our table, towards the back, where I am now, I looked around to see who was in then as well…and as I glanced towards the door area, I saw a chap standing there, talking to someone, who I thought looked an absolute spitting image of me. In fact, I nudged one of my friends and said, "Who's that over there?" …and he said, "Blimey…it's YOU!"

He even wore the same sort of clothes as me, which was incredibly spooky (if I may use that word)…and I said to my friends, "I think I'm going to have to go over there…"

…and after a bit of deliberation, I got up to go…and then as I did, I realised I couldn't see him anymore.

I made my way quickly over to the door, and sure enough…he'd gone.

It was one of those times that I so wish I'd moved faster and hadn't pondered.

A chance missed…never to be had again, I'm sure.

I would've loved to have seen his reaction too when I stood in front of him…he was honestly my double!

As I waited for my food, I sat there thinking about what Carla had said today…and thoughts of the can falling off the table onto the floor from the night before came into my mind.

That was really quite something…and I started to wonder about what he really could do if he wanted to. Boy oh boy, like I've said before, that table is quite a weight.

Charlie soon came over with my meal, and he sat down opposite me and asked me how the opticians business was doing as he felt his trade was dwindling slightly.

I said that it was slow for me at the moment too; and that I put it down to people generally thinking more about holidays at this time of year, and that they wanted to hold onto their money for that rather than buy new specs; or in his case, eat and drink out. To be honest, the optical business wasn't that quiet as people were buying sunspecs FOR their holidays, but I had to come up with something to make him feel a bit easier…I could tell he was a bit worried. I think it was a good reason anyway that he could justify why his trade had slackened slightly.

I liked Charlie. He was your typical London landlord, full of charm and banter; and even though he was slightly perturbed, he quickly agreed with what I'd said, brushed it all aside and was leaning back in his chair and interjecting conversational jokey comments to the couple behind him…that was Charlie: a truly great character!

I left the pub around 9:00 p.m. and headed back to the flat. I fancied some more of that raspberry ripple ice cream, so I went straight down to the kitchen when I got back and took out the tub from the freezer compartment of the fridge.

"Evening, My Scary," I said as I took the lid off, whilst turning around to look behind me and back down the corridor.

I was feeling quite relaxed with the food and drink I'd just had, but a certain nervous part of me had still kicked in to make me aware of things.

I opened the cutlery drawer as I scanned the work surface, looking for the dessert spoon.

Where did I put it?

I searched around in the obvious places, but it was nowhere to be seen.

…hold on…I walked back into the living room and started looking across the carpet…

Well…he's done it once, so he might do it again.

"OK, OK, I give up…where have you hidden it?" I said out loud.

I stood there in the middle of the living room, looking everywhere and anywhere.

"Oh come on! Where is it?" There was a slight reserved tone of anger but definite frustration in my voice, as I knew this was probably one of his 'games'.

I was looking in ridiculous places now…under the cushion, under the table…I even went back into the kitchen and opened the bottom cupboards to take a look…but no, nothing!

Well, that was really strange. I know for sure I wouldn't have put it anywhere different to where I normally do, and I knew the last place I used it was in the kitchen when I tucked into the ice cream on Saturday lunchtime…and I was pretty sure that I didn't venture further than the kitchen either, just having a few mouthfuls before I went out.

Oh well…I gave up in the end, grabbed a tea spoon instead and went back into the living room with the ice cream and sat down on the sofa.

Jackie had some music playing downstairs, a bit of Def Leppard if I'm not mistaken…and although I loved disco and funk music, I really liked rock stuff too.

BANG! BANG! BANG!

Blimey, I almost jumped out of my skin! Someone was knocking on the door!

I got up and went down the stairs.

It was Jackie, with music blasting out behind her.

"Christine is here, and others are coming over later…"

She said it in a 'so you need to be down here too' type of voice, which made me smile…but it did sound a good idea anyway.

"Yeah, that's great, Jacks. Give me a minute or two, and I'll be down,"

She had quite a lot of these impromptu-type parties. Well, I say impromptu, she probably did plan them, but they just seemed to happen out of the blue to me, which was great. But because of her phlegmatic, laid-back nature, she often had the wool pulled over her eyes; and unfortunately, that happened at the beginning of the year…

We both had planned New Year's Eve parties in our flats at the same time.

I had lots of friends coming down from outside of London, and Jackie had invited a load of her normal crowd.

All was going superbly until around 11:30 p.m. when one of my friends in my flat was showing concern about what was happening outside my front door in the hallway and told me to look down the stairs, through the glass, over the door. When I did, I couldn't believe what I was seeing…it was just a sea of heads!

I immediately went straight down the stairs, opened my door, and I was met with a horde of people, clutching cans and bottles of beer.

I could see that Jackie's door was wide open, and her flat was absolutely HEAVING.

I turned and walked with purpose, down the steps to the concrete stairs, passing more and more people along the way; in fact, there were people all the way down the passage and right to the front door…which was (surprise, surprise)… WIDE open!

It felt like half the population of the town was in here!

I stormed out onto the road where as luck would have it, a little Mini Metro police car was just driving down. I ran out into the road and flagged it down. The two policemen inside were like Laurel and Hardy in stature. Hardy (the larger one) wound down the window and received my instant stream of babbling about the gate crashers, and that I wanted them out.

I remember him saying, "Calm down, sir," as he and Laurel followed me into the side passage way, with me marching in front of them, pointing at people saying, "I don't know him! …I don't know her! …I don't know him!"

We went up the stairs, and I pushed myself into Jackie's flat, shouting, "Jackie! Jackie!" trying to get myself heard.

She then suddenly appeared amongst the throngs of people as I shouted for the music to be turned down.

She stood there looking at me; her expression one of bewilderment as I pointed and ranted on about the 'hundreds' of people everywhere, strongly expressing my concern to the situation, as all the people booed and jeered at my verbal tirade and gesticulations against them.

...and then...she said it...

"It's OK, Steve; they said they're all going to go after midnight."

Oh boy! I can see Hardy now as he gave me a 'you're wasting our time' look, and then he turned to Jackie and said,

"So what you're saying then, madam," and then, he slowly looked back to me again, with the same look, and then back to Jackie, "...is that you're happy with all of these people in your flat?" ...and Jackie replied with a complete non-concerned tone of voice...

"Yes... they're all going to go after 12 o'clock."

Hardy exhaled deliberately at length, then looked at me and said,

"Well, then there's nothing we can do, sir."

"NO, JACKS... NO!" I shouted...I couldn't believe how relaxed she was about it all, and I remonstrated with Hardy, but he and Laurel just turned and walked away and back down the stairs, leaving me getting an absolute onslaught of verbal abuse from the cheering jeering crowd.

I unlocked my door and stormed back upstairs to my flat.

I was so bloody angry and frustrated, but I had to clear it out of my head as the time was getting on, and I had my own planned 12 o'clock party celebrations.

It was around 12:30 a.m., after seeing the New Year in with Auld Lang Syne and a lot of dancing, that I went over to the stairs and looked down through the window again...

There was no one there.

I walked further down the stairs, opened my door and went out into the hallway.

Jackie's door was wide open. There was no music and all was quiet.

I walked inside and saw just seven or eight people standing there, talking. One was Christine, and she came over to me when she saw me...

"Blimey! ...they all did go then," I said in complete disbelief as I gave her a kiss and wished her a happy new year.

"Yeah, but you won't believe what they did, Steve," she said, pointing, "Look, they've kicked the plug sockets off the walls, and they've taken Jackie's TV!"

I COULD'NT believe it!

"WHAT!" I said. "They've taken the bloody TV?"

Jackie heard my raised voice and came out of the kitchen. She looked totally unruffled, completely calm and placid, as she always was, as she wandered up to me and said...

"It's OK, Steve...I never really watched it anyway..."

"JACKIEEEEE! ...for god's sake!"

Oh boy, I was so cross. I didn't want to say I told you so, and I didn't...but I so wanted to!

Jackie was so untroubled to the point of being annoying!

But that's the way she was...nothing EVER seemed to ruffle her feathers.

What I could never understand though is how they got the TV out of the flat and down the stairs without any of Jackie's true party-going friends seeing! Because apparently, they DID NOT...and it wasn't a little portable, like my Grundig...it was a big heavy 26"!

Back to June...

Dolly turned up with her brigade of moon and star followers around 10:00 p.m., and it turned into a really good party. If there was anything going on upstairs in my flat, this time, I certainly didn't hear it due to the party noise...although Christine did catch my attention now and then, as she put her hand to her ear and glanced to the ceiling with a funny look on her face...little devil!

I stayed there until around 1:00 a.m. and then went back up to the flat for a quick bath and bed.

Everything seemed strangely OK...I could sense the muffled feeling as per usual, but the atmosphere seemed lighter, though I do not know why.

I still did my patrol 'of the grounds', looking for any signs; but thankfully, there were none to find.

Wednesday, June 25th
Going Around in Circles

I woke up just before the alarm went off and made my way into the bathroom to brush my teeth and have a shave.

Everything seemed fine again in the flat, well…other than the water that was scalding hot as usual.

It also crossed my mind that I didn't wake up at 3:00 a.m. again either as I walked back into the bedroom and pulled back the curtains and got dressed.

I went down into the kitchen and put the kettle on for some tea and opened a cupboard to get out some Weetabix. I put a couple in a bowl, poured in some milk with a shake of sugar and looked for a spoon.

Ah yes, NO spoon…this is ridiculous, I'm going to have to get myself some more cutlery.

I looked again through the drawer for the dessert spoon, hoping as if by magic, it had put itself back in there…but knowing full well that Mr Scary had done something with it…and I DID believe that too as I couldn't think of any logical explanation as to its whereabouts.

I think if I had had other dessert spoons, I wouldn't have paid so much attention to one going missing; but as it was my ONLY dessert spoon, and the fact that I now had to use a tea spoon to eat my cereal, it DID flamin' matter!

"Oh come on, where've you put it for god's sake?" I said irritably out loud.

I took my bowl and tea spoon through to the living room and sat down at the table. I pulled up the hanging table cloth slightly and looked underneath again…well…you never know!

Eileen was in today. She was working her normal Wednesday and Thursday, now that Carla was back from holiday.

As I made my way down to the practice, I opened the side door and there she was, sitting there with a cup of tea, pointing to one that she'd made me that was sitting on the workbench.

"Come on, what's your news…I was going to come up and knock on your door…"

She had a big smile on her face, and her eyes were wide open as she continued eagerly, "What did Carla say about your flat?"

Eileen had a very precise pronunciation of words; which almost came across as being posh sometimes. She'd say words like 'theatre' as 'thee-arr-tarr', which always made me smile. But when she got excited and wanted to know something…like she did now…her accent almost became East End!

I told her how Carla wanted to go up into the flat, and how she had come running out of the bathroom, like a bat out of hell and back down the stairs.

Eileen was almost smirking at my re-enactment, and we did have a little laugh about it; but she was concerned for Carla, and I reassured her that she was OK. I said how Carla reckoned that it was just a mischievous spirit who wanted to play games, and that she also thought that it wouldn't be around for very long. I never mentioned Carla's rethink though that it might have a hidden agenda!

Eileen listened to it all and then gave me 'her look', and I reassured her that I too was alright…and I was…sort of. Mr Scary DOES scare me, and I'd be lying if I said otherwise; but I knew that in my mind, I was in control of it all…well, like I say…sort of.

It was really odd living the way that I was living at the moment, but I knew I could handle it.

In a very weird and unusual way, I think I was kind of enjoying it!

Eileen added that even though I was trying to put her mind at ease, she was still concerned for me and felt that I should still have a talk with Mr Barnes, to tell him what was happening.

I had no real intention of doing that though…I couldn't see any point in it…and to what purpose? It's not like he was going to provide me with alternative accommodation, and I certainly couldn't afford something separate myself…and to be honest, I would've felt absolutely silly, telling him anyway.

I know Eileen had mentioned it to him last week, but she had only asked whether there was any history to the flat pertaining to spooky occurrences…I'm sure she wouldn't have given any indication as to my state of play with it all; that's not how Eileen does things.

Eileen was like a mother hen to me all morning. If I had said yes to all the cups of coffee she offered me, I think I would have been best working from the toilet!

At 1:00 p.m., we closed the practice and went over to the pub on the corner for some lunch.

I had sausage and chips whilst Eileen had a 'light sandwich' as she called it, and we sat and talked the hour away. It was funny, but we never really ever spoke about work much during our occasional lunch time get-togethers. It was always about Eileen's family and her home life, or my so-called 'love' life…with a lot of Eileen's advice and direction thrown in for good measure, of course.

I compare that with conversations with work colleagues of today, and more than likely, we always end up talking about something to do with work, as today there seems to be so many more issues with working life. Back then, we seemed more calm and relaxed. We cared about what we did, and how we did it still, but we weren't moaning all the time because we didn't have senior management breathing down our necks with immoral, non-realistic targets; whose only concern was to meet and beat those targets by whatever means!

Ah…the good old days, as my father would say…and his father before him I'm sure…

We did wander onto the subject of the flat as well, and Eileen expressed her concern AGAIN; and this time I really did try to reassure her that I was coping with it all, and also that I didn't feel I should speak to Mr Barnes for the reasons that I'd said earlier.

She said she understood and added that she hadn't really mentioned anything to him in detail anyway about what was going on. (I knew she wouldn't…good old Eileen.) She also went on to say that he had shown quite a level of interest though, and that I should be prepared that he might start talking about it when he next called in to see me…thanks Eileen.

We headed back to the practice just before 2:00 p.m., sucking on our Polo mints.

Eileen put yet more coffee on, and we settled in for the afternoon's business.

The working day soon came to an end without any issues, and we were out in the back office, getting ready to leave.

"Are you doing anything tonight that you can tell me?" Eileen enquired with a wry smile on her face as we closed the side door of the practice.

"It's going to be that exciting that I probably will be able to tell you EVERYTHING," I replied, with a laugh.

She laughed back as I walked her down the side corridor.

As I opened the door, Jackie was about to come in with Johnny.

I said goodbye to Eileen and beckoned them both through.

"Helloooooo Jacks…and how's you Johnny? Good day at work?"

Jackie gave me a big hug, and John had a funny look on his face as he replied with a: "could've been better for me…and for you!"

I looked at him with a puzzled look, and then it clicked as to what he was referring to…

…the car auction!

I'd forgotten all about it.

"…you won't believe what happened…" he continued as he walked ahead of me down the corridor.

…and I was thinking to myself, "I probably will…" as it had all sounded much too good to be true to me anyway.

We went into Jackie's flat, and John ran through the story…

Apparently, there WERE just two other bids as he had envisaged. One was a silly bid, then came my oh-so sensible £501 bid, and then came a crazy £1250 bid…which, of course, won the day!

John said that the man that bid the winning amount was the chap that was going to bid the £500, but he panicked and upped it rather a lot and now feels 'bloody cross' when he found out how much less he could've got the car for. Mind you, he's still got an amazing bargain though!

John kept apologising to me, and I could tell he honestly believed I was going to win it.

Blimey, it certainly would've been superb if I had of done…but that's the way it goes.

It's funny how over the years, things like that have happened to me. You could call me 'The Nearly Man'. I'm smiling as I type this, as I can relate to many experiences where I feel that I really got very close to something amazingly good in my interpretation, but I just didn't quite reach it for one reason or another…hmm, anyway, that's all by the by…

John didn't stay long, and he soon left…it seems he only came around to tell me the car news.

I actually felt more disappointed for him!

I think he really felt like he'd let me down, and I made the point of saying that I hadn't banked on winning the car, and that the auction had actually slipped my mind anyway.

I always felt with Johnny that he wanted to do good for the people that he knew, and I think he genuinely gets a kick out of making those people feel good too; and I guess that's why that when he left, he did look quite down in the mouth, even after all my reassuring.

Jackie offered me some food for tea, but I fancied going next door to the wine bar, so I thanked her anyway, then made my way upstairs to the flat.

I walked out onto the living room floor and did my usual greeting and scouted around the rooms.

I noticed the atmosphere seemed rather heavier than usual, especially as I walked down the corridor and into the kitchen.

I could feel it changing as I walked through. It was almost like I'd passed through a doorway about halfway down the corridor…I could feel the 'air' alter…my whole body tingled…it was really odd.

I turned and walked back up to the living room; and as I did, I felt the alteration again as the feeling disappeared, and it all suddenly went back to 'normal'.

I stood there looking down the corridor. I wanted the experience again. I felt the urge to go back down to the kitchen.

As I walked past the bathroom, I felt the sensation once more. I could feel a tingling pressure against my face, like static electricity, which almost felt warm and the feeling seemed to increase as I entered the kitchen. I stopped and stared. I wasn't looking at anything; I was just experiencing the sensation on my face. Then suddenly, a flickering caught my eye; and I focused immediately in front of me. I found myself looking at the blank wall opposite the cupboards as I blinked a few times.

I just stared, and as I did, I could see patches of grey forming against the wall. They were like very faint, long and thin, smoky wisp-type shapes…almost like a projection against the light cream colour of the wall. I stepped back slightly towards the cupboards and was leaning against the kitchen top. I just kept staring. The shapes were soft and curvy and seemed to be moving slowly in a circular pattern as they faded in and out. It really confused my sight, and I kept blinking whilst I adjusted my specs in a disbelieving manner. I kept staring as gradually, one by one, they faded away.

I walked forward towards the wall where the shapes had been. Was that just me doing that? Were my eyes acting like a film projector?

Some people are aware of 'floaters' in the eye, which are actually microscopic bits of debris that float around in the vitreous humour between the intraocular lens and the retina. They cast shadows on the retina, giving the impression that they are floating in front of the eye, almost to the point where you feel you can reach out and touch them.

Was this what I was experiencing?

I don't think so, but it was an explanation of a sort.

I started to feel a bit dizzy, so I made a conscious effort to walk back up the corridor to the living room again.

Almost immediately, my head cleared…and I felt fine again.

Blimey! Now that was very weird…

I stood there looking down the kitchen corridor. I felt slightly bewildered…I wasn't sure what had just happened really.

I interlocked my hands on my head and then slowly turned and looked around me and back down to the kitchen again.

Should I go back down there? I wanted to…I wanted to see if I could feel the change in the 'air' again.

In the warm summer months, when I was living with my parents, I would often go out for a 'blast' around the village on my motorbike, wearing just a t-shirt and shorts (against my father's advice)…and I remember the alteration in air temperature as I rode. I could feel the change against my skin really clearly as I rode from one air pocket to another…and I remember turning around on some occasions and riding back along the same stretch of road, so that I could experience the change in air temperature again.

This was something like that…

I put my hands on my hips for a second as I thought about what I was going to do…and then, I slowly walked back down the corridor to the kitchen…

Nothing happened this time. No tingling or strange feelings at all.

I walked back to the bathroom, and I pushed the door open a little further than it was, and stuck my head inside.

Nothing! I knew there wouldn't be anything in there either, and I felt absolutely unruffled about it all.

I went back to the kitchen and looked at the cream-coloured wall again; my eyes moving up to the ceiling and back down to the work surface…and then, I just stared at the centre of the wall again.

I wanted the shapes to reappear! What were they? Why was Mr Scary doing this?

Now that was a stupid question really, because why was Mr Scary doing ANY of this?

Mind you, this was really different…and I'll tell you why…

I felt so at ease…so relaxed and calm. I wasn't scared at all…in fact, totally the opposite. I felt like nothing could bother me. I felt completely tranquil…almost spaced out!

Is this how Jackie feels all the time?

That thought made me smile to myself as I walked back through to the living room and sat down on the sofa.

I looked down the stairs, but I wasn't really looking. My eyes were open, but my mind was doing the seeing. I was just staring into space whilst I chewed over what had just happened.

I leaned forward and looked to the right, down the kitchen corridor again.

I realised I was feeling reasonably back to normal again…my head felt like it was back on my shoulders, and I could think straight.

That was really quite an odd experience.

The best way to describe it to you would be if you could imagine that you'd had a couple of drinks and that you were feeling a little merry and light-headed…and then suddenly, those feelings were taken from you in an instant, and you were stone-cold sober again. That would be the best comparison.

…and yes, I knew my normal senses had definitely returned, as my stomach was now reading me the riot act!

I went into the bedroom and removed my work clothes, then walked back down the corridor to the bathroom. I stopped at the doorway once again and held my head high, slowly looking from right to left, expecting something…but receiving nothing.

I went inside and had a quick 'splash' in the sink to freshen up.

I've mentioned having a splash before, and I still do that to this day. A 'quick splash' equates to running the cold tap and using soap on my hands and face, then splashing my face with the water using cupped hands, and then doing the same over my head and hair like a mini head-shower.

Mind you, the water goes everywhere, but it certainly freshens you up no end…especially with cold water too.

Almost every time I turned the hot tap on in the bathroom, I would forget just exactly HOW hot the water was, and today was no exception. I jumped back, pulling my hand away when the scalding temperature registered on my skin. I swear it seemed to be getting hotter too, and this triggered me to walk around to the immersion cupboard for yet another 'look'. And I wasn't checking the switch anymore…I was more concerned about the state of the tank. It will be glowing soon at this rate.

I returned to the bathroom and finished off, then back into the bedroom to get some clothes on.

I walked out into the living room as I fastened my jeans and looked down into the kitchen again. Then I returned to the bedroom and put on a t-shirt, grabbed some money and came back out onto the living room floor and looked into the kitchen once more, as I knelt down to tighten the laces on my plimsolls.

I couldn't get it out of my head what had just happened. It was so weird and strange, yet I felt excited.

I think I said earlier that I was almost enjoying the experience of what was happening to me in the flat; although, perhaps, 'enjoying' is a bit strong.

…and I know that might sound absolutely ridiculous, considering everything that I've told you that's happened so far; but as it went on, I was beginning to find it all rather compelling, and this latest episode was certainly not scary to me at all. In fact, it was more intriguing and thought provoking, and I felt myself being completely immersed in the whole thing.

It also made me feel even more sure that he wasn't going to hurt me, and that he was just mischievous and wanted to play 'games', like Carla had said.

…and he certainly had quite an array of games too, and I think that is what was so enthralling…what game was next?

I know what you might be thinking though…Carla had said about this so called underlying agenda, a false sense of security and all that…but I felt fine about it all, and I wasn't thinking on those lines as I stood up and walked back down to the kitchen ONE last time.

Right!…it's definitely all back to normal…so finally, let's go out and get something to eat!

I locked my door and turned to look into Jackie's flat through her open doorway.

I wanted to tell Jackie about what had just happened, but I was hungry…AND I was going to phone my parents tonight too!

"See you later, Jacks," I shouted out.

I heard her say something in reply from within as I bounded down the stairs, but I couldn't quite make it out.

I hesitated outside the practice side door, but I carried on walking down the passageway…I'll phone them when I get back…it's terrible, my stomach was well in charge!

The wine bar was incredibly quiet.

I had the place practically to myself, and the Italian owner came over and passed the time of day with me…

"Buona sera!"

He was your typical Italian restaurant owner…very loud and flamboyant, with an accent that almost sounded like it was false and put on, but I knew that it wasn't…well…I hope that it wasn't!

There were so many times he'd stop in conversation, look to the ceiling and say… "…ow d'you say…?"

I never had any of the Italian dishes though. It was always something like a big jacket potato with prawns and melted cheese, mmm. That probably sounds very boring, but I've never really got into Italian food. I've always said that I could just live on snacking too. A bit of something here one minute, then back for something else half an hour later.

It's 11:30 a.m. on New Year's Day, as I write this at the moment…and I've just had a big handful of peanuts as I drink my coffee…nothing changes!

It's funny, but when I was in the wine bar, I always had a glass of wine rather than a beer. It just seemed to be the right thing to do. I almost felt like I would be roughing it if when I was asked, "And, can I getta you a drinka?" (best Italian accent), that I requested a lager.

Perhaps it's the posh bit of me coming out, or the part of me that just wanted to blend in with the crowd more like…that is, when the crowd is in here!

In the late 70s, I was into the punk scene; so blending in was far from my mind then. I wanted to be different and to not conform to mainstream ideas.

I would often go to disco's at the local village hall with my friends. They'd be dressed in their wide-collared cheesecloth shirts and flares, whilst I would be in my tight black drainpipe

110

jeans, with a slashed black t-shirt, expressing my liking for a particular punk band at the time, called The Vibrators.

I'd wait until a punk record had been requested (two if lucky)...then the dance floor would suddenly clear, like the parting of the waves, and myself and perhaps two other 'hidden' punks in the hall would suddenly appear and start pogoing around the floor. The trouble is, the DJ never really put on anything truly punk. I can remember making the most of 'Dancing the Night Away' by The Motors one evening, as that was going to be the nearest we'd get!

It was always odd when the record had finished too. It would always go silent, and I would walk off the dance floor, sweating for England, with my two newfound punk 'mates', with looks on our faces that said, "Right, that's our bit done for the night...you can have your dance floor back now!"

...and it did feel like that too...for as soon as we'd trudged off, the disco music would be put on again (with the DJ making some snide comment about what had just taken place)...and then, the dance floor would fill up once more as if it all had never happened.

Actually, I can remember once when 'God Save the Queen' by The Sex Pistols was put on by a DJ, who had a terrible sound system. He had it on so loud, it was distorted almost beyond recognition, but hey...it was proper punk!

"Buonanotte!"

I left the wine bar around 8:30 p.m. and went for a walk around the town. I thought I'd check on my car and made my way around to the church...

Good, she was still there and in one piece.

I did my circuit of the shopping parade and made my way back to the flat.

I MUST phone my parents! I let myself in the side door of the practice and spent half an hour having a natter...but I still didn't mention all the flat stuff that was going on...not on the phone. I was going back 'home' at the weekend anyway, to host a disco for my friend's cousin's 21st birthday party, so I'd be staying over and having Sunday lunch with my family; so I might tell them then.

I reset the practice alarm and went back up to the flat.

Talking of alarms! Boy oh boy, let me tell you this. One day, leading up to Christmas last year, I'd spent the evening in the flat, playing some music and generally relaxing and went to go to bed around midnight.

When I'd turned everything off, I was aware of an alarm ringing away outside, and I went to the bedroom window and looked 'sideways' through the glass to see if I could make out where it was coming from. The alarm from the shoe shop further down the road was always going off, and I immediately assumed it was that; and I got into bed, turned on the radio and dozed off.

At around 2:30 a.m., I woke up and could still hear the alarm sounding off down the road, and I remember thinking to myself, "Bloody hell, this is ridiculous, someone should have turned it off by now!"

I went back to sleep and woke up around 8:00 a.m. and was immediately aware that the alarm outside was still ringing. I couldn't believe it they'd let it go ALL night!

I had some breakfast, got ready for work and left the flat.

As I walked down the concrete stairs and got closer to the practice, the alarm sound got louder and louder and LOUDER...and yes, as you've already guessed, it was the OPTICIANS' ALARM! ...ohhh, bloody HELL!

...I remember panicking to open the side door and rushing in to punch in the alarm code...and then, standing there absolutely motionless in the blissful silence as I contemplated what I'd let happen.

I just couldn't believe it! I'd let it ring ALL BLOODY NIGHT!!!

WELL!

...I had to lie and lie and LIE to save face throughout the day, with seemingly every local resident coming into the practice to complain.

"I was out all night and just got back this morning...I'm so sorry!"...that was the line I gave each time.

*Even Jackie said (and remember she was living right **above** the practice!) that she had wrapped her pillow around her head all night, trying to sleep as she thought I was out too!*

Oh blimey, I really felt absolutely TERRIBLE! ...but I never let on.

Anyway, I'm digressing again...

It was about 9:00 p.m. when I got back to the flat.

Jackie's door was now closed, and I could hear her music playing away as I unlocked my door, switched on the light and went up the stairs.

I greeted Mr Scary, then went straight to the tape player and turned on some music.

I glanced around the living room. Everything looked fine and where it should be as I walked down the kitchen corridor and into the bathroom to use the toilet.

I started to think about what had happened earlier. There were certainly no strange feelings down the corridor anymore, but I was still wary as I moved around.

I went into the kitchen and poured myself an orange squash, then went back into the living room and sat down on the sofa.

It's funny, but I imagined Mr Scary to be all around me now.

I thought of him looking at me as I sat there, watching my every move.

I looked around the room.

I always looked up high to the ceiling and the corners. I guess that was because of the height thing experience in the kitchen, I suppose. I always imagined now that if he was going to be anywhere, it would be there.

My mind was working overtime as I sat there, sipping my drink and visualising his face coming out from the walls!

I know that sounds crazy, but after this latest happening with the 'shape' thing from earlier, I would say anything is possible in this ruddy flat!

And I think that was what the trouble was. I was looking for things to happen. It's like you can almost feel you can make something happen with the power of imagination…with the power of the mind.

It's like going to see a film, let's say *Superman*, then coming out of the cinema and thinking you can fly.

Of course you cannot, but you imagine that you can!

I read a book last year that my father had given me, called *Wild Talent,* which was about a boy who had the gift of telepathy and telekinesis. My father had read it years ago when he was a lad and said that I would find it interesting…and I did.

Even from school age, I would often mess around, trying to make objects move in my bedroom just with my mind…and I always hoped that one day I would really be able to do it…that if I practised hard enough, the so-called unused part of the brain might suddenly kick into gear…and it would actually happen!

Well…I had long forgotten all about my interest in telekinesis, and those frustrating attempts to be able to perform it; but after I had finished reading the book, my curiosity in the subject was once again relit, and I spent much time, on and off, trying to fulfil the dream.

It's like my fascination with UFOs. I can forget all about them for a while…then I'll pick up a book on the topic, or see something on TV pertaining to it, and before you can say, "Is it a bird? Is it a plane?" I'd have my eyes to the skies once more.

I sat there for a while, thinking and listening to the music, and then I decided to run a bath and have a soak.

I needed to clear my mind.

I was most certainly thinking too much about the evening's events, and a bath with some music sounded a good way to remedy it all.

I picked out a tape, rewound it and pressed play and then got in the bath.

I had the bathroom door pushed wide open and held back with my kitchen bin.

I know that sounds unnecessary, especially as the door didn't NEED holding back; but it certainly made me feel a whole lot better, knowing that there was something there that could prevent the door from swinging shut. That is if Mr Scary decided he wanted to do that. Mind you, a little lightweight kitchen bin wasn't going to stop him if he really wanted to close it, I'm sure, but it made me feel easier anyway.

I know, I know, I'm being paranoid; and I'm sure that to someone looking in from the 'outside', I certainly was. But it did lighten my thoughts doing odd things like that. It was the same when I greeted him and spoke to him too. It was just my way of dealing with the situation.

I climbed into bed around midnight and went straight to sleep.

Thursday, June 26th
Not Jock'ular

I did wake up just gone 3:00 a.m. because I can remember looking at my clock; but after a brief, strained listen to the silence, I turned over and went back to sleep.

I beat the alarm again by 5 minutes; and as I lay there, I smiled. I was dreaming shortly before waking, and it was all suddenly coming back to me in my mind. I was sitting outside someone's house, in a brand new Ford Granada (I've said goodbye to the Rover already!), and I was waiting for them to come out…and I was excited in anticipation of them seeing the car!

Isn't it funny how the mind works…

I remember, a few years before I moved to the town, I had a spate of dreams that actually came true, and unfortunately, there was one in particular that got me into a rather awkward situation.

It happened when one night I dreamt that the opticians practice where I was working at the time was going to be burgled, and when I went into work the next day, I mentioned it in jest to one of my colleagues.

A few days later, I walked into the practice in the morning as usual through the back door, only to be met by the Police who were investigating a break-in from the night before…gulp!

That work colleague had said to them what I had mentioned to him a few days before, and they were obviously keen to speak with me. Thanks for that!

Thankfully, this 'seeing'-into-the-future type stuff came to a halt…and probably just as well.

Both Eileen AND Carla were working today.

It seemed ages since we'd all been in together, mainly because of Carla being on holiday I suppose, and I was really looking forward to it.

I made my way down to the practice a little earlier than usual, to get things ready for the day.

When it was the three of us working, I tended never to get a coffee ready for Carla first thing as it didn't feel right doing it for just one of them. Though I can remember on one Thursday just for fun, I had a mug of coffee, tea and a glass of water sitting on a tray waiting for Eileen so that she could take her pick!

They both walked in together today (almost like they had planned it) at about 8:40 a.m.

"Have you been a busy boy then?" said Carla, in her cheeky manner as she hinted as to whether I'd set everything up in the practice for the day…knowing full well that I had done!

Eileen was checking her reflection in the long mirror and hand-brushing down her skirt. It was like a ritual every morning with them both as I sat there sipping my tea and now watching Carla giving her dress a good going-over too.

With clothing adjustments accomplished, and with coffee in hand (coffee for Eileen too this morning), we all sat down on the brown plastic office chairs, pulling them closer together in a homely huddling kind of way, and we started chatting.

Carla always looked up to Eileen. (And, I don't mean in height, as they were both around 5'4.) She would often say things that would be in admiration of her…and it would be said in a way that always gave me the impression that she was hoping that one day her life would be like Eileen's.

Eileen always had a sort of air about her. I think I've mentioned before that she almost came across as being slightly up-market, though I knew really that she was very much down to earth. She often mentioned social events that she was going to be attending or had attended, and I could see in Carla's eyes that they were functions that she would love to go too; but that deep down she knew she never would.

She lived it out through Eileen's descriptive wordings though, like she lived out my weekends, with a mischievous, playful, almost teasing smile, that disguised her desire for perhaps more.

She would often comment on Eileen's experiences, with an "Oh Eileen, you ARE a little devil"… to which she would always get the shaking head from side to side response,

"I'm not Carla, I'm not," which always made me laugh, before I added something too.

They both asked about the flat, and I told them of last night's kitchen occurrence.

"He's just playing with your mind…" responded Carla rather swiftly, and she went on to reassure me again that he was just a 'playful spirit'.

Eileen also reiterated her concern once more and added that she would've moved out a long time ago!

"No worries tonight anyway, I'm out for most of it."

I was meeting some friends up in Covent Garden for a drink, and then we were going around to the Hippodrome in Leicester Square afterwards. I'd been there for the first time a couple of months back, and I was really looking forward to going again.

It was an expensive night out but well-worth it for the atmosphere and the music.

The working day went by rather rapidly. We were incredibly busy at times, and I spent most of the lunch hour with a patient who took a month of Sundays to make her mind up!

We closed on time though at 5:30 p.m., and we all commented that it was good that we'd had the chat first thing as we really hadn't had much time during the day.

"Have a good time tonight, see you next Wednesday," said Eileen as she walked down the passageway after I'd set the alarm.

"It's going to be quiet tomorrow, Steve…we've got no clinic booked!" added Carla as she hot-footed after Eileen…and I was pleased with that really, as I knew I'd get back in late from uptown; so with no clinic going on, hopefully it wouldn't be too busy.

"Thanks a lot both of you…bye!"

It was a good job they both had been working today too; I think it would have been too much for one of them.

I walked up to the flat and opened the door.

I think I might have come over as being a bit nonchalant to Carla and Eileen as regarding the goings on, but as I walked up the stairs to the living room I can tell you now, I was as wary as ever!

Everything seemed fine though as I grabbed some money, and then made my way back downstairs again. I was going straight around to the Tun's for a quick drink and a bite to eat and then off up the West End on the train.

Charlie greeted me from the bar as I walked through the door. The place had quite a few people in for this time on a Thursday night, but no one that I knew.

I ordered scampi and chips, with a pint of Tennant's top to wash it down, and I sat at a table by the back wall.

I stayed there until around 7:00 p.m., then headed back to the flat to get ready to go out.

I put an LP record by Shalamar on the disco unit, turned it up and went into the bathroom for a quick splash. I felt in a real party mood tonight, and I was dancing around as I got changed.

I was soon ready; and after checking I had enough £10 notes in my pocket, I made my way down the stairs.

"See you, Scary Boy…don't miss me too much."

My mind was occupied with thoughts of later on tonight uptown, and I think that definitely made me feel mellower with Mr Scary. I was still very aware of the atmosphere as I jumped down the stairs, but I was quite pumped up with thoughts of the night ahead OUTSIDE the flat!

I caught the train just before 8:30 p.m. and arrived at Charing Cross in a twinkle of an eye.

It always amazed me how really close I lived to the heart of London.

I walked through to Covent Garden and made my way around to a clothing store called Flip. It was a good a place as any to meet-up, and I had a good opportunity to look around while I was waiting for my Hertfordshire friends to arrive…and I knew they'd be late anyway…

We went to a bar, which was a favourite of mine. It was situated below ground level and reached by a metal spiral staircase. Around the sitting/drinking area were barrels full of monkey nuts, to which patrons were invited to help themselves and take a handful back to their table.

Once eaten, the remaining shells would then be traditionally shoved off the table and onto the floor.

You'd be walking/kicking around on a carpet of monkey-nut shells, which was a really weird experience but fun.

After a few hours chatting and drinking, we made our way over to Leicester Square and into Stringfellow's Hippodrome around 11:00 p.m.

The last time I came here, I left my drink on a table to have a dance; and on returning, found that it had been taken…and at £2.50 for half a lager; that's no joke.

I was more wise tonight ('second time around' and all that…Shalamar rules!), and I made sure I finished my drink before hitting the floor.

At about 1:00 a.m. (and they did this last time too), they put on an amazing visual 'show' where 'robotic aliens' in silver suits descended from high above the dance floor while jets of dry ice and coloured lasers shot everywhere, as the pumping beat of *Two Tribes* by Frankie Goes to Hollywood base bounced through your chest! WOW! …it was really superb.

The only trouble with all this was, the dance floor had to clear to allow it to all happen. (Yes, I know, my turn to leave the floor.) And although it was fantastic visually, you couldn't actually dance to any of the music, well…you could…but you didn't…you just stood there and stared for ten minutes or so at the spectacular. It was really quite something though.

I left The Hippodrome around 3:00 a.m.; and after saying goodbye to my friends, I walked back down to Charing Cross to look for a taxi. I knew they'd be a group of drivers standing around at the back of the station with their cars. They were not licensed cabbies, but they would take you to where you wanted to go for an agreed fixed amount of money.

Trying to get eye contact was the hardest thing! I remember this from last time…it's like they can't really be bothered!

I spoke to the nearest driver to me, and he responded as if I'd asked him to take me to China! I felt rather awkward as I went from one driver to another. Each one responding the same as the first, until finally one of them said, "See, Jock, he'll look after you."

I looked in the direction of his pointed finger and saw a tall, big, dark-shape of a man, standing in the shadows, who was smoking and looking down at the ground as he leant against the back wall. The collar of his heavy black leather jacket practically concealed his face, as without looking up; he took one last drag on his spindly cigarette and threw it on the floor. He then blew out the smoke, hesitated, mumbled, "Ten…" and then made his way over to an old, dark-coloured Ford Cortina…

Well…I just followed…I was feeling desperate…I wanted to get home.

I got in the back of the car on the passenger's side and reassuringly felt in my pocket for my money. Good.

I wanted to clarify where we were going again as we drove off, but I didn't.

I wanted to clarify the fare again, but I didn't.

I just sat there, looking out of the side window and occasionally glancing at him.

After a while, I had to say something, "Have you been busy?"

He never replied…not even a flicker of acknowledgement.

It was a bit disconcerting really, and it made me instantly re-evaluate the position I was in.

He may not have heard me I suppose, but I'm pretty sure he must have done.

He's probably just tired, and doesn't want any early-morning small talk.

…and he doesn't have to talk, does he? It's not like it's compulsory.

It would certainly be a much better atmosphere in here for me though if he did say something…

Tower Bridge was approaching.

Good…we're going in the right direction…that made me feel a bit easier.

I was looking out of the side window again, but my attention kept being drawn back to him.

His collar was still up, obscuring the side of his face, and even the rear-view mirror was at a funny angle, so I couldn't really see him properly that way either.

He looked more of a Ford Granada driver to me though; he was much too big in stature for a little old Cortina. His head was practically against the ceiling of the car whilst his body enveloped the seat below him.

I kept looking at his side profile.

Blimey, there was something certainly strange about him.

I wonder if he knows Mr Scary?

That stupid thought made me recoil slightly.

My mind was running in over-time now.

WHY did I have to bring Mr Scary into it?

I sat there, looking out of the window front and side and then back to Jock.

Bloody Jock!

There were no body language giveaways…no twitches, no glances back, no grunts, no nothing!

I just sat there apprehensively, watching London go by…

"Can you drop me off just along here please," I said pointing as we thankfully approached the top of the shopping parade.

Jock responded by slowing the car down to a stop and I got out. Phew!

I went around to his side of the car and offered my money against the glass.

The side window was ablaze with reflected lights from the estate agents as I tried in vain to view the face within; and then suddenly, he drove off.

I stood there motionless with the money in my hand as I watched him drive away and turn the corner. What? Did I pay him at Charing Cross? I'm sure I didn't; in fact, I know I didn't. I walked down towards the practice side door. I was almost expecting him to come back around the corner again, but I could hear the car accelerating away in the distance. I punched in the key code and quickly opened the door, pushed in the light plunger and shut the door behind me. Blimey, I could feel the relief in me that I was home. He certainly was a weird one, and so odd that he drove off without taking my money. I'm sure he must have seen me holding the £10 note against the side window!

I walked up to the flat, unlocked the door, turned on the light and walked up the stairs.

I stood still on the living room carpet as I looked around. The same old closed-in flat feeling was present, but I also had a strange feeling that Mr Scary had just come back from somewhere too.

I know that sounds ridiculous, and you're probably thinking that I'm associating it with the cab driver, and that is probably true, but I did feel that as I walked onto the living room floor, that Mr Scary had returned with me.

I cannot explain it properly other than saying it was just a feeling, like you've just been out with someone, and you've both come in together…very odd I know.

I'd better get to bed…it's just gone 4:30a.m!

Friday, June 27th
Dust You Wait and See

The alarm went off. I certainly didn't beat it this time, and I was amazingly up with a start.

I turned the radio on and went into the bathroom and ran a bath whilst I brushed my teeth. The water came out boiling hot as per usual, and I walked over to the airing cupboard again, with brush in mouth, to have another look. I don't know why I had to have a look almost every time…but I just had to.

A quick soak, then a slice of toast with strawberry jam for breakfast, followed by a swift iron of a shirt, and I was ready for the day.

I walked downstairs around 8:40 a.m., and after turning off the practice alarm, I immediately filled up the kettle and switched it on. A few minutes later, I heard the side front door bang, and the distinctive sound of Carla's heels coming down the corridor.

"Morning, handsome!" she said as she barged through the ajar side door, with her early morning shopping bag. I was stirring the coffees and turned to see her grinning face looking at me.

"Oh boy, look at you!" she added as her head went back like a boxer avoiding a punch, "What time did you get in last night? You look half-dead!"

"Thanks, Carla!"

I was feeling OK, I thought…just a little bit tired I suppose; but obviously, my face told a different story.

She unpacked some food stuffs from her bag and put it in our little back office fridge and sat down with her coffee.

"You could have a sleep in the consulting room this morning, Steve. Catch up on some Zs. I'll wake you if anything exciting happens."

I shook my head, "No way, Carla. I'm fine. This coffee will keep me going."

Well, we were so quiet business wise. Not a soul came through the door; and by 10 a.m., I conceded that I was feeling rather tired, and that I would take Carla up on her offer and have forty winks in the consulting room.

"Please wake me up, Carla, if I'm needed."

"Yes, yes, I will," she said. "Go on, go and get some shut eye."

I knew it was wrong, but the spectacle checking-in work was all done, and because I was still in the practice, it seemed to make it alright. Carla could quite easily come and get me anyway…it wasn't like I was going to go back upstairs to the flat and go back to bed. That's how my mind saw it anyway…I felt I could sort of justify doing it this way.

I adjusted the consulting room testing chair to lean well back, got comfy and nodded off.

WELL!

The next thing I knew, I opened my eyes, looked at my watch…and I was absolutely horrified!

It had just gone 3:00 p.m.!

I jumped out of my consulting-room 'bed', opened the door and stuck my head out to look down the practice.

There was Carla at reception on her own, with her head down, writing away.

"Carla!" I said, with almost a tone of annoyance, though I, of course, didn't mean it that way as I walked down towards her.

"Why didn't you wake me up…look at the flamin' time!"

"You were out for the count, and we've been absolutely dead, so there was no need…"

Oh boy. I felt so guilty.

I kept thinking about Mr Barnes, and if he had walked in…now that wouldn't have looked good.

Carla was laughing as I kept airing my concerns of what could have happened.

"You were snoring for England in there; I had to close the door."

She made me laugh.

I went out into the back office and put the kettle on.

It was a practice that went from one extreme to the other. If we had no doctor working with us like today, we could be so quiet that occasionally I would go and check the practice door to make sure I'd actually unlocked it!

Then on a day when there WAS a doctor working, we could be run off our feet. There was never any middle ground.

Carla came out to the back office.

"Stop worrying, Steve…it was OK; nothing happened."

"I know, I know…but it could have…"

We sat and chatted.

She wanted to know more about The Hippodrome, and I duly obliged.

I didn't mention anything to do with Jock, and how I felt when I got back to the flat; and to be honest, Carla never asked about the flat stuff anyway. I think she was deliberately not asking, probably leaving it up to me if I wanted to say anything.

It was nice just talking about normal things again really.

"Chris phoned by the way while you were in the land of nod. He said the princess would like to see you later if you were interested? Does that make any sense to you?"

I laughed, "Yes, it does…and I am interested."

Carla over-exaggerated the raising of her eyebrows as she sipped her tea.

"He meant the Princess of Wales PUB before you start thinking anything," I said, with a big grin.

"You don't have to make any excuses to me, Steve," she retorted quickly, with a little wink.

I liked Carla's sense of humour. She was always a little bit cheeky, with a constant play on words that always kept me on my toes. Eileen was the same really, only a little bit more reserved than Carla.

I'll certainly miss them both when I leave.

We locked up on time with everything done and prepared for Saturday.

I walked Carla down the corridor as usual.

"See you tomorrow, Steve…and just you be nice to that princess now…" she said as she reached the passage front door.

"I certainly will," I replied, "and I'll try and be much nicer to you tomorrow too…and keep awake!"

When I paused mid-sentence, she had stopped opening the door and had turned back to look at me with her eyebrows raised, and an expression of jokey anticipation on her face. This soon changed into a broad smile when I finished the sentence, and she continued opening the door.

I walked back along the corridor and up the concrete steps.

I don't know what made me look, but as I rounded the top steps, I glanced up to the windows of the flat, and I noticed what looked like a crack in the far left pane, that was reflecting in the sun.

I stood there on the spot, looking up at it. That's really odd; I don't recall that being there before, and it looked like rather a large split too.

I walked into the flat hallway, unlocked my door and walked up the stairs.

I immediately went over to the living-room windows and sure enough it was a crack. It must've been about a foot and a half long, spreading from the bottom right-hand corner into the middle.

"Have you any idea how that got there?" I said out loud as I turned back around; my eyes scanning from left to right.

Damn it. I suppose I'm going to have to report that to Mr Barnes.

It looked fairly safe though. It didn't look like the pane was about to fall out.

I went over to the tape player, put on some music and then walked into the bedroom and got changed out of my shirt and trousers.

I can hear it all now.

"So how did you manage to break it then, Steve?"

Hmm…I think I'll leave it for the time being.

Mind you, I was blaming it on Mr Scary. It could have quite easily been caused by something else…

I went into the bathroom to freshen up.

It felt strange in the flat tonight.

Now I know that's a daft thing to say as it's been VERY strange in here for about the last two weeks! But it felt like the air was charged again. It was a bit like the feeling I had on Wednesday night, down the kitchen corridor, only I could feel it all the time; and it seemed much stronger.

I could feel a tingling against the skin on my chest and shoulders as I walked from the bedroom to the bathroom and back again. I stopped and brushed my chest with my hand as if I was removing biscuit crumbs, and it was gone. But as I moved again, the tingling returned, and I could feel a very slight bristling sensation on my arms, and I could see that the hairs were standing up.

Something is going to happen, I could feel it…it was building up.

I opened my wardrobe door and took out a t-shirt that was lying on the inner shelving.

OWW! I got a big static shock in my fingertips as I unfolded the shirt.

WOW! That was quite strong!

I carefully picked up the shirt and walked into the living room, and then I stopped still and stared.

The sun was streaming through the windows and was creating a huge angled pillar of sunlight effect that had illuminated all the fine dust particles floating in the air.

But what had caught my eye was what some of the dust particles were actually doing.

They were swirling around slowly in the middle of the room!

I just couldn't believe it! There was this dust particle circle of about two feet in diameter, just revolving there; about five feet away from me in mid-air; about five to six feet off the carpet.

It was like a cigarette smoker that had blown a rather large smoke ring; only it was quite faint.

I was absolutely rooted to the spot, watching this unbelievable event.

It faded in and out slightly as the sunlight diminished and strengthened, but I could see it continue to revolve as it started to move very slowly towards the dining table…and then…it suddenly broke up as I lost sight of it, as it moved out of the sun's rays…and it was gone.

My goodness! That was amazing! Absolutely breath-taking.

I stood motionless and just stared back into the sunlight at the normal moving dust particles as the brightness and warmth of the light quickly faded as the sun retreated behind a curtain of cloud, as if signifying the end of the performance, and the living room suddenly became 'normal' again.

WOW! That was incredible…and it was all over so quick.

My heart was pounding, but not through being scared. I was just in awe of what had taken place.

Boy oh boy! That was almost angelic…

I remained perfectly still, hoping…waiting for an encore.

Please do it again…

Then suddenly, the curtain went up as the spotlight was turned back on again.

The dust particles were visible once more but doing nothing abnormal as I slowly pulled on my t-shirt and then went back into the bedroom to put on some jeans. I then came back out into the living room and stood there, looking into the shafts of sunlight again. I was spellbound.

Did Mr Scary do that with his finger? That was the thought going through my mind.

I realised I was standing there staring with my mouth open, and I quickly shut it.

I moved a couple of steps forward and put my right-hand index finger out in front of me and turned it around and around as if I was drawing a circle in the air.

I smiled, as the very fine particles of dust just scattered everywhere in the sunlight, and I immediately stopped and walked back into the bedroom to put on my plimsolls.

My mind was buzzing.

I walked back out into the living room again and just stood and stared into the rays of light once more. I was turning over in my mind what had happened. That really was quite incredible.

I felt like I had just experienced something really magical. It was nothing threatening or worrying; it was just amazing…and now I actually felt incredibly warm inside. It was like someone had said something really heart-warming to me, and I was glowing from within.

I stood there, just staring into the light rays, still hoping for the encore. Would he do it again? He knows I want him too, so there's no chance!

I looked down at my left forearm and rubbed it. The tingling sensation had gone, and the air felt back to normal.

I glanced around the living room and then back over to the crack in the window again.

There's certainly never a dull moment!

I realised how thirsty I'd become and walked down into the kitchen to get a drink. The flat lemonade almost tasted good, as I stood there, looking out of the kitchen window and down at the passing traffic below. I turned and glanced at the wall above the kitchen top. No, he likes a bit of variation; he certainly wouldn't repeat himself.

I walked back up the corridor and looked around the living room again.

I still felt incredibly good in my mind. I know it's an odd thing to say, but that's how it was. Like I said, I really did feel like I was glowing from within, and I felt completely at ease with things in the flat.

I could not stop thinking about the swirling circle, and I was looking forward to telling John and Chris.

I was soon walking up the road and making my way to the pub.

I could see there were already a lot of people sitting and drinking outside on the grass, across the road; and as I got closer, I started to scan the faces, looking for familiarity.

I soon heard, "Stevie boy!" and I saw John walking across the road to meet me.

"I was going to give you until 8:30 p.m., then I was going to knock you up."

"Where's Chris?" I enquired as I looked back across the road onto the grass.

"He might be coming later; he's got something to do first."

…well, this was a first for me, seeing John on his own. Chris was always with him!

"Come on, let's get some drinks!"

So, with John clutching his empty pint glass, we went into the pub.

We got a couple of beers and sat down in the pub, and slowly I enlightened John with all my latest goings-on in the flat.

He just kept swearing in disbelief, and we sat there talking about it for most of the evening. He apologised again about the car auction result; but otherwise, we talked mostly about the flat.

He re-aired his hypothesis again of us letting the thing out of the attic; and I must be honest, I think that is the only explanation. I know it sounds so far-fetched, but if you take everything into consideration that has happened in the past two weeks in the flat, I would say it's probably the most plausible.

We did have a laugh about the swirling circle. John reckoned Mr Scary was trying to write something in the air to me. Well, if he was, it began with O!

Chris never turned up in the end, and we left the Princess at closing time and walked back down to the flat for a coffee. Johnny said that he was looking forward to seeing if he could experience anything, which made me feel quite good. I actually started to feel excited myself that he might do, but I knew deep down that he probably wouldn't.

I opened the flat door, turned on the light and walked up the stairs; giving John, who was a couple of steps behind me, a running commentary.

We got to the top, and I turned on the other lights and had a quick look around. Everything seemed normal and in the right place.

John laughed at what he described as the 'serious look' on my face when I did my scout around.

We were both a little merry I would say but totally in control.

"Now stand still Johnny and tell me how the atmosphere feels to you in here. Does it feel closed-in or woolly?"

I suppose I shouldn't have used the words 'closed' and 'woolly', as if I was feeding him the lines; but John said he felt OK, and that everything seemed normal to him.

I was disappointed again as I was when Carla came up.

"Don't you feel sort of muffled in your head?"

"I ALWAYS feel like that!" he replied very quickly, and we both laughed.

He looked up at the attic hatch.

"There it is then; the gateway to Spooksville!"

I looked up at the hatch too.

"We should get that open again; you never know, it might decide to go back up," said John, with a grin on his face.

"Don't you feel anything strange?" I persisted rather frustratingly.

John put his hands out in front of him, palms up, like he was checking for rain and walked over to the disco unit. Then, he turned around and looked at me.

"Nope; not a thing." He then walked over to the entrance to the kitchen corridor.

"Go on, walk down," I said eagerly as I turned on the kitchen light and ushered him forward with my hand.

Come on, Mr Scary. DO something!

I watched him walk down the corridor.

"Bloody hell, this is what we heard in Jackie's last Saturday," he said as he looked down at the sloping floor that was creaking beneath him.

He stopped by the kitchen window and slowly turned to meet my awaiting stare from the other end of the passageway.

He raised his eyebrows and pulled a face as he shook his head from side to side.

Oh, come on, Mr Scary...please...just this once!

I walked to the bathroom, pushed open the door and turned on the light.

"See if you can feel anything in here."

Johnny walked back up the corridor and pulled a face at the creaking floor again and then gingerly entered the bathroom.

He looked around the small room, like an estate agent, then exclaimed, "Yardley GOLD!" as he pointed to my after-shave, sitting there on the shelf.

"They had no Armani," I retorted very quickly.

He gave me a big grin.

He stood still as if taking it all in, then turned around and came back out.

"Sod it; I really want to feel something!"

He was smiling as he said it, and it made me laugh. He had urgency and frustration in his voice though, and I knew he really did want the experience.

I made a coffee, and we sat down in the living room.

He started to go on about the car auction fiasco AGAIN, and once more, I told him that it didn't bother me and to stop worrying about it.

Johnny always came across as a decent bloke, giving the impression that he cared for everyone. This was the first time too

I'd been just solely in his company for an evening, and I really did like him more for it.

(He came along to my wedding, in later years too.)

I knew he had another side to him though. I'm pretty sure he had connections with London's underworld, although he never admitted it or spoke of it. It's funny; but even tonight, being in his company, it never crossed my mind to ask him about it. I think we all just accepted that he had this other life.

I told him that I called the ghost 'Mr Scary', and he was the only person to ever know that. It was Dolly that instigated the name, but I never continued it in company. Even with Eileen and Carla, I just referred to it as the 'ghost' or 'him'.

And it was only in the flat that I actually said the name out loud.

John laughed when I told him and said that he knew of another 'Mr Scary'; though his Mr Scary wasn't a ghost.

He never elaborated…and I never inquired.

"Do you know what, Steve, this is the first time I've been in your flat, and you haven't put any music on?"

I looked at him for a moment, and then I nodded my head in agreement.

It was true. It was the first thing I would always normally do when I walked into the flat, but I suppose it was the Mr Scary thing. He'd changed me and my routine quite a lot.

I remember one evening when I was living with my parents, I'd returned from somewhere to find that they had friends visiting, and that they were all talking and drinking in the living room. I stuck my head around the door to be sociable and said, "Hello," and then went upstairs to my bedroom.

The next evening when I came home from work, my father come up to me and said with a smile, "You let us down last night, you know!" I responded with a puzzled expression on my face.

"The first thing you always do when you go upstairs to your room is to put your music on loud, and I'd told Bob and Alma that, and I was saying, wait for it, wait for it! …and you never did!"

Well, Dad, actually I did put it on, but quietly; BECAUSE you had your friends there... They just didn't hear it...at my 'normal' volume!

After John had gone, I went straight to bed.

I lay there with my hands behind my head, staring up at the ceiling and thinking.

The flat seemed almost normal tonight.

Perhaps I need to get company around more often!

Saturday, June 28th
Let the Spirit Flow Free

I slept right through and woke up literally just before the alarm and lay there contemplating the day ahead.

It was going to be a busy one, and I wasn't just referring to downstairs in the practice either.

I was doing another disco again tonight. This particular one was for a friend's cousin's 21stbirthday, which was back over my parent's way again, and I was staying over for the night at theirs too. I'd planned to leave just after we closed the practice at lunchtime, as my mother was going to cook me a dinner, and I wanted to spend a few hours with my family before I went back out again.

I was soon up and ready and was at the big table, having some cornflakes for breakfast.

I sat with my back towards the window and kept glancing around the room as I eat.

The flat always seemed very calm and relaxed in the mornings. The muffled feeling was there, but like I've said before, it was never as obvious as when returning to the flat after being out somewhere.

I finished up, said my 'goodbyes' for the morning and then went downstairs to the practice around 8:30 a.m.

I prepared the doctor's room and checked reception, made Carla's coffee and myself a tea and then sat myself down in the back office.

I soon heard Carla's heels coming up the passageway…

"Ooooh, you are good to me, aren't you!" she said as she spied her coffee sitting there.

"Gotta keep the troops happy," I replied with a big smile as I raised my mug to her.

She was wearing a bright-yellow, blue-spotted short dress, that really made her look browner than ever as she sat herself down, crossed her legs, picked up her coffee and looked at me expectantly.

"Well?" she said, with a big smile.

I knew what she wanted to hear, but I made out I didn't know and looked around the room with a thoughtful expression.

"Come on, Steve. What are you up to this weekend?"

It was our Saturday protocol.

"I'm doing another disco, would you believe?"

"What!" she exclaimed, "It'll be your full-time job soon, at this rate!"

It was just a coincidence doing two in two weeks…and anyway, I'd be much too nervous doing it all the time…mind you…

Just before I moved away from my parent's house, I did an audition to be a resident Saturday night DJ at a night club in a neighbouring town.

It was a joke really, as the nearest I'd ever got to operating a 'proper' club disco unit was my own FAL Disco that I had now, which was very basic and easy to use; just having slider up and slider down for volume, with a bass and a treble knob!

It was a Sunday night, and they'd only opened the club for the auditions, with a few invited guests of the owners, who were probably just there for the free drinks.

I went and sat with the other DJs; as one by one, we were called up to do our thing.

"Can we have DJ Steve, please!"

Gulp…I climbed the stairs to the 'disco area', which was up in the rafters at this club, and I can remember my thoughts of horror when I saw all the knobs, switches and dials. I can also remember the look on the chap's face that was 'looking after us', when I asked him if he could give me a quick overview on how to use the flamin' thing.

"You are joking!" he said in a tone of voice that really said, "What the bloody hell are you doing here?"

Well…as you can imagine, my audition didn't go down particularly well.

I managed to get the records playing, but my 'voice over' was so quiet because I didn't have the volume correct...and basically, all I said was the title of the record and then I bottled out.

I can remember looking down at the two 'judges', who were sitting on chairs on the dance floor and seeing them lean towards each other and mouth something with rather negative looks on their faces.

Hmmmm...they kindly let me last for two records before the chap standing with me took the microphone and said, "Well, thank you...that was DJ Steve!"

I was so nervous, and as I went back down the ladder and walked out of the club, I tried my hardest to avoid any eye contact with ANYONE!

"DJ Steve has left the building!"

I love Saturdays at work. Most patients want new spectacles, and generally, everyone is in a weekend mood...plus, we close at 12:30 p.m. for the day, which is superb, and today it seemed to fly by quicker than ever!

Carla was all chirpy as we stood in the passageway outside the side door, ready to go and waiting for the practice alarm to set.

"I'm being restyled at 3 o'clock, Steve," she said as she shook her hair back, like a model in a TV commercial.

"I'll be a new woman on Monday; you'll never recognise me!"

I laughed.

Carla was referring to her hair, of which she had the same Farrah Fawcett look since I'd known her; and to be honest, it suited her; and this time, I knew it would be no different.

"You'd better make sure that you're wearing trousers or tights then, so I'll definitely know it's you!"

She was walking in front of me, and she stopped and looked back...

"You'd never get me in tights Steve, stockings perhaps...but never tights."

I laughed again.

I think she knew what I was getting at, but we were at the door now, and she was wishing me a good weekend...

"You too, Carla; see you Monday."

I walked briskly up to the flats, unlocked my door and ran up the stairs.

I sensed the same old closed-in feeling as per usual, and I did my quick look around before going into the bedroom and getting out of my work gear.

I had a quick splash, put on some shorts and a t-shirt, and then started to pack an overnight bag.

I never really packed much when going back to my parents. Pants, socks, a different T-shirt and some jeans for the evening…then my shaver, anti-perspirant and after-shave; but that was about it.

I still had my own toothbrush back at home too.

The important 'packing' to do was all the records. I always felt like I was in a record store when I did this, as I flicked through them all one by one, looking for the floor fillers of the evening.

I soon had my dance favourites in a couple of record carry cases, and I placed them in the middle of the living-room floor. Then, I unplugged the disco speakers and put them in the middle too, followed by the leads and headphones in a carrier bag. Then I went and got my overnight bag from the bedroom and placed that there too. I couldn't help it; I was always very methodical like this when I was taking stuff somewhere. I liked to stand back and look at it all, and make sure I hadn't forgotten anything.

Right! I was ready to rock and roll! Well, get funky at least.

I grabbed my keys and made my way down the stairs and over to the church to get my car. My eyes were scanning the parking area as I got closer. Phew, it was still there.

I drove down to the road outside the practice and bumped the car up the pavement right outside. It was always a nightmare doing this at this time of day, with so many people around and cars driving through, but I had no other choice.

I opened the side door and ran up the passage way and up to the flats.

I stood there with my hands on my hips, looking at the stuff to go.

Did I put Michael Jackson's *Thriller* in? I know I did, but I had to check again.

I kneeled down to open the case…

GUUUUSSSSSSSSSSSSSSHHHHHHHHHH!

I stopped dead still…

GUUUSSSSSSSSSSSSHHHHHHHHHHH!

What the heck was that?

I jumped up and moved towards the sound.

It was coming from the bathroom.

I moved towards the kitchen corridor.

It was so loud!

GUUUUSSSSSHHHHHHHHHHHHHHHHHHHHHH!

I pushed open the bathroom door and was met by a cloud of steam. I grabbed the light cord and pulled it.

My god, there was steam everywhere. It was like a sauna, and I immediately saw where the noise was coming from. It was the sink. The taps in the sink were on full blast!

I grabbed the tops of them with each hand and tried to turn them back, but they were locked hard.

The water was gushing and rushing and splashing, with the hot water making me pull my hand back every now and then because it was so damn hot as I wrenched at the taps. I was really panicking, and I couldn't work out which way was off. I tried turning one way, then the other way. TURN OFF! TURN OFF! But they wouldn't! They were locked on hard!

Then suddenly, they turned like they had just been released, and I turned them back as fast as I could until they were shut.

Then, it was suddenly deathly quiet…

I stood there looking at the sink through my steamed-up specs.

Bloody hell! That was crazy!

I stepped into the corridor and took off my glasses and wiped them clear with the end of my T-shirt.

I put them back on and looked into the bathroom.

The steam was subsiding as I went back inside and put one hand on the cold tap and slowly turned it on. Water came out as normal, and I turned it off. I did the same with the hot tap, and then I just stood there looking.

What was that all about?

They had been on FULL!

He'd actually turned the taps on FULL and stopped me turning them back!

I walked into the living room. I felt kind of numb. I was staring at the stuff in the middle of the room but not really 'seeing' anything…and then suddenly, my mind switched into gear!

BLIMEY! MY CAR! I'd better get down there.

I picked up one of the speakers and made my way down the stairs.

As I came out of my doorway, Jackie was walking towards me, coming back for her lunchbreak.

"Hi Steveeeee. Are you alright?"

She said it with a concerned look on her face, as she obviously read the anxious look on mine!

I put the speaker down and blasphemed and animated my way through a quick account of what had just happened whilst she stood and listened.

…and then Jackie said the immortal line that has stuck with me for all these years.

"Let the spirit flow free," and she intimated that I should open the windows front and back before I go.

I laughed and gave her one of those looks that says, "Thank you, but no thank you," picked up the speaker and made my way down to my car and spent the next five to ten minutes going backwards and forwards, loading it up. The disco deck was always the most troublesome. Not because of its weight, but more of its size and getting the thing actually IN the car.

Right! I was loaded and ready to roll.

I stood on the living-room floor, having a last look around, and then I thought about what she had said.

Oh what the heck, let's do it.

I pulled one of the dining chairs over to the window in the living room, climbed upon it and reached up to the top window.

Blimey, I hadn't opened this since I'd moved in, and it was really stiff. I pushed and banged it and finally it opened…and I set the catch.

I did the same with the top window in the kitchen and then hurriedly put the chair back by the table.

I then went back into the bathroom and checked the taps again.

I just had to do it one last time.

Right, I've got to get going before I get a parking ticket.

I looked up at the open window in the living room as I descended the stairs, and I said out loud with a lot of sarcasm,

"Let the spirit flow free!"

…and I smiled to myself.

I shouted out "See you, Jacks" through her open doorway and ran down to the car.

I know it sounds daft, but as I drove out of the town, I actually remembered that I hadn't said my normal goodbyes to Mr Scary…and it did make me feel quite odd inside to the point that I almost contemplated going back.

Crazy I know, but hey…these were crazy times!

The journey over to my parents was quite slow. It always was on a Saturday afternoon. I only really managed to put my foot down when I got through London and made it onto the M11…and I spent a lot of the trip thinking about what had happened in the bathroom.

Why was there so much steam? Was it because the hot water was so ridiculously hot, and that it was being mixed at force with the cold water? Probably.

I did keep thinking also about how the taps were being 'held' open by Mr Scary, and that was I really fighting with HIM to turn them off?

It could have been me, in my panic, getting confused as to which way actually the right way was to turn them off. I know that sounds silly, but in the heat of the moment (if you'll pardon the pun), I think I might have even jammed them myself!

Anyway, the one thing for sure was that they had been turned on, and they were turned on FULL! …and there was no mistaking that at all! …and there was only one explanation in my mind for that happening!

I spent the afternoon with my parents and my brother and two sisters.

My mother started on a liver and bacon dinner, with mashed potatoes, onions and gravy, as soon as I got in… Mmmm.

She said she was doing a big roast tomorrow, which I was DEFINITELY looking forward to.

I still never said anything to them about Mr Scary. I'm not sure why. Possibly because, like I said a while back, my mother would worry herself silly and would be phoning the practice every other day to see how I was. My father I'm sure would have

140

just thought I was 'losing my marbles'. I think he would be probably concerned though, but more to do with the state of my mental health than anything else.

No…I still wanted to keep it away from my family at the moment.

The disco/party went well.

It was a very strange set up though. I had my disco deck in one room, with the speakers in another. It was a good job that the unit had long speaker leads, otherwise I think it would have been a bit of a disaster.

It was great fun though, but very odd listening to the music playing in the 'distance'.

I received a round of applause when I mixed Michael Jackson's *Wanna Be Startin' Something* into *Thriller*. There's nothing special or difficult about the mix, but it was great to hear the cheer…from the other room!

Sunday, June 29th
Let's Clear the Air

I came down at about 10:30 a.m. on Sunday morning to a smoke haze that had been produced by my father, who was sitting at the dining table, with a big mug of tea, puffing away at his pipe. My mother soon appeared from the kitchen, offering to cook me a fried breakfast.

"It won't spoil your dinner, will it?"

No chance! Boy, I was famished.

I leaned against the kitchen-door frame, watching my mother cooking egg, bacon, sausage and beans as they both quizzed me on my life in London.

I was soon pulling up a chair at the kitchen table and eating my mother's late breakfast offerings, accompanied with my own big mug of strong tea…superb!

My brother and sisters soon surfaced, and it felt like I hadn't ever been away.

It was almost my coming home ritual that after dinner, we would move the dining table into the living room and set it up as a makeshift table-tennis table, using Ladybird books as a net. When we got bored with the books constantly being knocked over, and the various arguments that ensued, we would place a portable quarter size snooker table base onto the table (which lived behind the sofa) and continued with that instead…and these games would go on and on, only ever being interrupted by my mother's afternoon tea and cake, which was always a bun-round, with a cherry in the middle, and then finally sandwiches for tea before I left to go back, which my father always liked to do. His speciality was his cheese and watercress sandwich, which he liked to call a 'Mysteron Sandwich' named after Captain Scarlet and the Mysterons that was on TV. Why did he call it that? Probably because it was actually on TV at the time when he was making it once, but it stuck for years…and today, when he asked me what I wanted, I just had to have it.

"Don't leave too late, Steve; you want to get back in the light!"

…my mother kept saying that from about 7:00 p.m. onwards!

I left around 9:00 p.m., with a great family send-off; all waving from the front door.

I got back just after 11:00 p.m.…and it was dark!

I parked the car outside the practice and unloaded all my stuff, taking it down the corridor and leaving it just outside the practice toilet whilst I went off to park the car.

On returning, I picked up one of the speakers and made my way up the concrete stairs and up and around to the flats.

I could see Jackie's light was on as I unlocked my front door, switched on the light and carried the speaker up the stairs.

As I stepped onto the living room floor, I stopped and put the speaker down…

Hold on! Things seemed different. I couldn't sense anything.

I walked further into the living room and turned on the bedroom light, then the kitchen light.

I stood still, cocking my head to one side as if I was trying to listen for something.

There was no heavy feeling!

There was no muffled feeling!

I walked quickly down the kitchen corridor, turning on the bathroom light and went inside…I could sense nothing!

Then, I went into the kitchen and doing a 360 turn, quickly walked back to the living room…again, I could sense nothing!

My head was clear. Where was Mr Scary? Had he gone? Had Mr Scary gone?

I looked up at the open window in the living room.

"LET THE SPIRIT FLOW FREE," I said out loud, with a tone of amazement and hopefulness in my voice

Oh come on! Surely, it wasn't as simple as that!

But at the moment, it certainly felt completely different.

My head was definitely clear…really clear…oh wow!

The woolly muffled feelings had gone!

I could feel the joy of relief rushing through my body as I started to believe.

Oh my goodness!

I ran down the stairs, pulled open my door with gusto and banged hard on Jackie's door!

"Jacks! Jacks! You did it...I think he's gone!"

She opened the door in complete bewilderment, like she had just got out of bed (sorry Jackie), as I grabbed her and gave her a big hug!

"Let the spirit flow free...that's what you said...I can't believe it. I think he's gone...I think he's REALLY actually gone!"

I was jumping around like a man possessed, or not as the case may be, but I couldn't help it. I was so over the moon, so overjoyed...it was an incredible feeling.

"I can't believe it, I just can't believe it! I'm sorry, Jackie. I feel absolutely incredible...it's amazing."

She laughed, and I mean really laughed as I hugged her again.

"I take it you opened the windows then?" she said as I released my grip on her.

"YES, YES...I did...and I think it's worked...I really think it's bloody worked!"

"I've never seen you like this before, Steve," and she kept laughing, "Do you want to come in?"

"No, no, it's OK; I've got to bring all my stuff up from downstairs...I'm just so pleased. I can't thank you enough...I'm sure he's gone; I really am...you did it!"

I left Jackie standing there, rather taken aback by my emotions and made my way quickly down the stairs.

Boy oh boy, I was flying high.

Had he really gone?

I picked up the second speaker and almost jogged back up to the flats...well, a fast stagger!

Jackie had gone back in as I lugged it up the remaining stairs and put it down on the living room floor.

Then, I stood there...absolutely motionless and cocked my head to one side as if I was listening again.

"YESSSSSSSSS!" I said out loud as I clenched my fist.

My whole body was smiling...the flat felt fresh. It was like I had spring cleaned it.

I ran back downstairs twice more to pick up the disco deck, records, and my bag; and after quickly depositing it all in the centre of the living room, I started to explore the flat like I was viewing it for the first time.

I walked into the bedroom, then all around the living room, then down to the kitchen, and then back up the corridor and into the bathroom. EVERYTHING felt so amazingly different; almost LOOKED different.

I cannot explain the feeling properly other than it was perhaps like I'd been wearing my motorcycle helmet around the flat for the last two weeks, and now I'd taken it off!

It was amazing…everything seemed to sound clearer…my footsteps, picking up a glass and putting it down on the kitchen top, shutting a cupboard door…it all sounded so different. It was like everything had been coated in some kind of sound absorbing material before, and now it had all been removed.

I made myself a mug of tea, and then brought it through to the living room and sat down on the armchair.

I was absolutely elated. There was no other way to describe my feelings.

I sat there and just looked around the room. And as I said, everything seemed to look different too. The walls seemed brighter, the orange colour on the sofa seemed brighter…even the carpet seemed a lighter shade, and I know this was all in artificial light too; but it really did all look enriched, more enhanced.

It may have been just my mind making it all seem like this, but it was like I had been wearing tinted glasses for the last two weeks as well.

I started to smile as I thought of myself walking around the flat, for the last two weeks, wearing tinted specs and my crash hat!

I kept smiling as I carried on looking around the living room, drinking my tea.

I just couldn't believe it…he'd gone…he'd really, REALLY gone!

I looked up at the attic hatch door.

Blimey, that all felt such a long time ago now…

What was the time? Is it too late to call Carla?

I got up and looked at my alarm clock in the bedroom. It was well past midnight…err yes, it was much too late!

I finished off my mug of tea and decided to have a bath before turning in.

I felt so overjoyed, I really did as I turned on the bath taps. The water came out still scalding hot, but I told myself that that wasn't going to change immediately anyway. What's the expression, 'It's not going to change overnight'. Well, in this case, it hopefully will.

I went back into the bedroom, got undressed, grabbed my tape player from the living room and placed it on the floor of the bathroom. I then crumbled in some bath salts, and after letting the water level get quite high, I turned off the taps and climbed in. I was thinking about the hot water tank and had deliberately used a lot of the hot water. In my mind now, the water temperature tomorrow would tell me for sure whether he had definitely gone or not. I was 99 percent convinced, but I always felt that he was involved with that too; and I just needed the water to be normal in the morning before I could truly believe that it was over.

I lay there, soaking and thinking, with the music playing.

I looked over at the mirror above the sink which had slightly steamed up, and I immediately thought of yesterday's full on tap encounter. Was that the last game? I felt sure it was.

I couldn't wait to tell Carla in the morning!

Monday, June 30th
Going, Going, Gone?

I had no 3:00 a.m. wake up and went right through until the alarm.

I lay there thinking for a minute about Mr Scary. Did all that really happen last night? Had he really gone?

I got out of bed and walked into the living room. There really was a different feeling everywhere. I know I always said that I could feel the heavy atmosphere more after I had returned to the flat, but I just knew everything felt different. It seemed calm and homely. It felt like it was mine again.

I went into the bathroom, turned on the light and squeezed some toothpaste on my brush and started brushing my teeth.

This was so good!

I wandered out into the living room as I brushed and looked all around.

Yessssss, I could feel it all just seemed normal, and I mean really normal!

I went back into the bathroom and looked down at the taps.

This was it.

I know it's ridiculous, but I was building myself up for this…almost stringing out the moment of truth.

I turned on the cold tap to wash my toothbrush and rinse my mouth, and then I hesitated as I looked down at the hot tap.

I put my hand on the head of the tap and slowly turned it open.

The water started to come out, and I tentatively put my fingers into the water stream.

It was cold…and then, it started to warm slightly.

RELIEF…absolute, total RELIEF!

I went quickly over to the immersion cupboard, opened the door and felt the tank.

YES…It was just slightly warm!

WHOO HOO! I flicked the heating timer switch back on and closed the door. Then, I turned around and looked up high to the attic hatch as I clenched my fists in front of me.

Surely, that was the end of it all…

Addendum

I remained living in the town for another three or four months, before I left to start a new job; and in those last days, nothing out of the ordinary happened at all. Everything, thank goodness, had returned to how it had been before Mr Scary's manifestation.

Eileen phoned me though shortly after I'd moved out to tell me that the bathroom ceiling in the flat had collapsed. She said that it had caused so much damage that the whole bathroom would need to be gutted and completely refitted!

I immediately thought of Mr Scary. Did he have anything to do with it? Of course, he didn't.

I'll tell you something though, I'm so glad I wasn't in there having a disco bath when it happened!

My new job was back over my parents way again, and they were happy for me to move back in with them (well, that's what they said anyway), until I could manage to sort out a new place of my own.

It was now June of 1987, and I had gone out for a motorbike ride with a friend of mine. We would often meet up for a summer nights drink and then have a blast around the lanes of the village…and it was towards the end of one of these rides that they came…

"I've never seen such a bloody clean bike!"

His words were laden with sarcasm as he sat astride his mud splattered machine, like a general about to go into battle.

My bike was better than clean anyway; it was immaculate. I was always polishing it. But in this situation, I suddenly didn't want it to be shiny any more. I wanted it to be dirty and streetwise like theirs.

His two 'soldiers' laughed and swore in approval of his ridiculing observation and excitedly over-revved their 250s, in a possible attempt to create acclamation sounds from their engines.

I felt uncomfortable. I didn't know where this was going.

They had approached us and instigated the dialogue, taking great pride in telling us that they were uninsured, untaxed and seemingly unbothered about anything.

We just listened and cautiously laughed at the right times, having an almost envious appreciation of these bad lads of the night...

Suddenly, his bald rear tyre revolved into life, spitting out dirt and dust in one fast short spurt of anti-social defiance.

"Let's race to Harlow!" he yelled.

It was a statement rather than a command, but we reacted. He wanted us to join them.

I looked at Mike.

He was already manoeuvring his Suzuki, and there was excitement in his eyes as he glanced at me.

We didn't know these lads; in fact, we were about to call it a night before they appeared on the scene; but here we were, about to go into highway battle with the nightriders...

We took off up the A11, like bats out of hell, with the bad lads shouting and screaming, like banshees, as they weaved their bikes from side to side in front of us, in a display of complete disregard to road use normality. We watched in disbelief as they cut through the intersection to ride the wrong way up the opposite side of the dual carriageway, then crossing back over at the next break to reappear in front of us again to continue with their crazy show.

They were mad, absolutely irrational, and we were being sucked into this fanatical early-morning charge by the exhilaration and anticipation, that was increasing at every second.

Wow! What a rush.

We soon hit a long straight piece of road, and I lowered myself down onto the tank. I was barely peeking over the top of the rev counter, in a vain streamlining attempt to keep up with them all as two-stroke smoke peppered the warm night air in front of me.

Come on! Come on! Faster! Faster!

My normal world of law abiding regulations, full of consequential thoughts and concerns, had vanished. I was now living completely for the moment. All that was significant lay directly ahead of me, in a one-way blinkered tunnel of sight and sound.

I wanted to go faster; I needed to go faster…

…and then suddenly…he appeared!

WHERE did he come from?

My soaring feelings of adrenalin pumping excitement immediately plateaued and dramatically fell into one of trepidation and panic as I saw that he was driving level with me on the other side of the road.

His outstretched motionless hand was a signal to stop, in fact it was more; it was telling me to go back. It was a strange feeling, but I knew that's what he wanted me to do. They were immediate thoughts, and I just knew.

I couldn't see him clearly, but he was there behind the wheel; a dark figure of authority, with a statuesque extended arm aimed towards me. It seemed to project an invisible line that I should not pass…a line that he did not want me to pass.

I kept looking into the car.

Had we almost stopped moving?

It felt like we had. Time seemed to have slowed right down. I was somehow connected with the car. I couldn't change focus. I couldn't look away. I must look away. I must look at the road.

"Go Back! Go Back!"

I slammed on the brakes and watched his car sling-shot ahead of me.

Did I hear him say that? It was a shout more than anything, and it certainly snapped me out of the hypnotic hold the car had on me. How could I have heard him? The passenger window wasn't down! Blimey, that was really weird, and I say I was connected with the car, I think it was with him. I felt the connection was with him somehow.

I watched as he sped after the others. He wasn't slowing…he didn't want me; he wanted to catch the bigger faster fish. I felt really odd as my mind subconsciously was analysing what had just happened, and how it happened. I couldn't have heard him; I just simply couldn't have!

I had come to a halt now, and there was just the sound of my bike engine ticking over as I viewed everyone disappearing around the bend in the far distance.

Was it an unmarked police car? Well, that's what I had assumed, and I felt relieved that I hadn't been officially stopped. I stared ahead down the empty road, almost expecting them to reappear and come charging back towards me. No, that wasn't going to happen, but something would; I had a strange feeling that something definitely would!

I turned around and rode slowly back home.

My head was buzzing with what had transpired over the last ten minutes or so. I felt I was jumping from one emotion to another. And now I was concerned…concerned about what was going to happen to Mike.

I cut my engine when I saw the lay-by and glided quietly to a stop. We always met and chatted here for a while after a ride, before going back to our respective homes; and tonight, I'm sure, would be no exception.

I sat and waited. After ten minutes or so, I started to listen more definitely for the distinctive sounds of his 250. He'd be along soon after his 'talk' with the police. I'd hung my crash helmet over the right mirror, had folded my arms and was impatiently listening into the calm early-morning air.

Come on, Mike.

I was feeling more and more agitated and unsettled. Should I ride back? There was only one answer to that, and I had already agreed with it.

I started the engine, put my helmet back on and rode towards the A11 and then onwards towards Harlow.

The only racing going on now was in my mind. Perhaps they'd all been arrested. Perhaps the nightrider gang were REALLY bad lads, and the police were now obviously assuming that Mike was one of them too!

I swung right at the second roundabout and headed towards the town centre. The roads were so quiet and deserted. Wouldn't it be superb if they were like this all the time?

That thought soon evaporated as I quickly focused on something going on further up the road. I could see a figure sitting on the kerb edge, looking towards me, which I soon realised was Mike. I then noticed loads of what seemed to be sheets of paper strewn all over the road as I tried to digest the scene that lay before me. Oh no, hold on...I've seen this before. I've dreamt this, I know I have...

There was a bike lying in the road, and another that was parked on its side-stand, which I recognised as being Mike's Suzuki.

He raised a hand in a dejected greeting as I pulled over. I glanced back down at the paper in the road again. Oh blimey, the 'memory' was so clear now. The paper was everywhere, and it was reflecting quite brightly in the lights from the yellow street lamps. I could see that there was also bits of plastic and metal intermingled, and I soon realised that they were bike parts.

I walked over to Mike with my hands out in front of me...

"You're not going to believe this, but this was in one of my dreams; it was just like this...all over the road!"

"That's our cancer and polio leaflets. My top box burst open when I came off...and thanks a bloody million for not warning me!"

(We did a money collection every two weeks going to certain houses, and some were a bit off the beaten track; so we used it as a good excuse to ride out.

The front part of the leaflet was always made glossy, and that was the bright reflection that I could see).

"And where d'you go?" he continued. "One minute you were there, the next you'd gone..."

Mike's tone of voice was one of annoyance. I did feel guilty for leaving him, and I definitely shouldn't have started talking with the dream. I knew that he was aware of some of the 'premonitions' that I'd been having over the past few years. But there was no way I could have prevented this. It only just came to me when I saw the paper everywhere anyway.

"I know, I'm sorry...the police car freaked me out. So what happened? Where are the others? Has he gone after them?"

As I was speaking, both our attentions were being drawn across the road to a car that had just pulled up, and the driver's window was being wound down.

"Is he OK?"

"Yeah, we're fine, no worries…thanks a lot," I replied in an overzealous, reassuring manner as Mike stood up on cue.

I knew Mike was alright; I just needed to get us away from here and back home.

"Do you want me to do anything? Do you need an ambulance?" said the rather nervous lady driver.

"No thanks, no honest, we're fine."

I could tell that she had only morally stopped, rather than for any genuine concern. She just wanted to get on her way, and her car was moving forward slightly in gear as she spoke. She soon drove off, edging slightly to one side to avoid the motorbike that lay in the road.

I immediately went over and pulled it back up. Blimey, it was in a right old state. The front wheel was completely bent in, the forks were pushed under the tank, and the rev counter/speedo mounting was non-existent. It was in a heck of a mess!

The wheels were jammed, so I slowly struggled dragging it a bit closer to the kerb and then let it fall back on its side, sort of half on, half off the road. It weighed a ton. I looked over at Mike. He'd sat back down again.

"Are you OK?"

"Yeah, I'm alright. Come on, let's get out of here," he said seriously as he stood back up again and walked over to his machine.

"Where's the bloke?" I said pointing at the wrecked bike.

"He went off with the others…"

"What?" I said with a completely puzzled look on my face.

"I know, don't worry about it…I'll tell you later," came the pressing response.

He pulled his helmet back on and started his bike.

"What shall we do about this?" I said pointing to all the paper and debris that littered the road.

"Leave it! Come on. I just wanna get back."

I restarted my Honda, and at a sedate pace we made our way out of Harlow and back down the A11. His bike seemed alright, thank goodness, but I could see him looking down at the tank every now and then as if checking something.

We were soon approaching 'our lay-by', and I wasn't sure whether he would pull in or not, but he did, and it was there that he told me about what had taken place.

Apparently the three nightriders were side by side racing in front of him, when one of them suddenly went straight over the handlebars like he'd hit a brick wall. Mike had braked hard to avoid collision and had skidded out of control and toppled over.

The crashed nightrider was in a bit of a bad way, and there was a mad panic to get him up and get him away from the scene. He managed to get on the back of one of the bikes, and they rode off towards the town centre.

"What about the copper? Wasn't he trying to stop them?"

It was at this point that we entered the twilight zone when Mike voiced that he had no idea of what I was going on about. I elaborated further; in fact, I went on and on about it. But he insisted that…

"There was never a car chasing us!"

Years passed by, and in 2008, I received an invitation to a retirement party at the practice for Mr Barnes.

I duly went and met up with lots of old faces from the past.

The opticians' ownership had changed hands, and I was introduced to the new owner who asked me whether I wanted to see upstairs in 'your old flat'.

He knew of my 'experiences' and wanted to know whether I wanted to have a look around the 'new' flat.

"You won't recognise the place now," he added.

He took me up there, and boy was he right.

It had been converted into an ultra-modern, ultra-slick bachelor pad. Wooden floorings were everywhere, with bright panelled walls and up-to-the minute swish fittings and fixings.

"Where was the attic hatch?"

"The attic was in such a mess, we decided to board it up," he said.

Lots of pigeons had gained entry, and it was not very pleasant up there.

Well there you go! Old Scary's original home had been boarded up for ever!

The new revamped flat was very nice, but it had completely lost its charm and oldie worldly feel.

I never said that to him, but I think my face might have done.

This now brings us right back up to present day.

I met my wife in Berkshire, had three children; and now, they're all practically adults themselves.

I'm living in a village in Somerset, and the happenings of those two weeks in 1986 are nothing more than a distant memory; and to be honest, that's fine by me.

We went on a holiday last year to a converted barn in South East Devon, just on the fringes of Exmoor.

It was a lovely, quiet place, set in glorious countryside, miles from anywhere.

It had an indoor swimming pool, table-tennis table, snooker table…wow, it was superb…and it kept us amused and entertained the whole week.

One evening, just as dusk was falling, I decided to take Gerry, our Bernese mountain dog, out for a walk, over the fields at the back of the barn.

I'd done this many times during our stay, and I'd worked out a route via three fields, that did not interfere with any of the livestock that were around.

I tried in vain this particular evening to get someone to come with me. My wife is not that keen on walking much, so I concentrated on the 'kids'.

"It's a clear sky out there, come on…we might even see a UFO!"

Not a chance! They had more interest in the TV, their mobile phones, and the comforts of the barn rather than going out for a walk across wet fields, in the rather blowy conditions of the Exmoor landscape…hmm!

"We haven't got any wellies anyway dad!" said one of my sons in an attempt I'm sure to appease himself for his lack of enthusiasm, but I was already down the stairs and looking for MY wellies.

I opened the front door, and Gerry ran outside like a gundog. He was holding his head high and sniffing the air as he started to make his way around the side of the barn, with me in hot pursuit.

We had soon entered the first field and were making our way into the second when I suddenly thought I saw movement in the hedges, far to the right-hand side.

I stopped walking and looked across. I stared, almost squinting in the failing light, to try and make out what I was looking at.

Was that a face? I blinked a couple of times and looked again. That was weird, I thought I could make out a face, but it was probably just the trick of the light…or the lack of it.

I started to look back and forth along the hedgerow, in a scanning type manner.

I turned and started to walk towards the hedge. I was intrigued. It was probably just a bird moving, but I felt compelled to get closer and see. The wind had now dropped, and the only real sound was the swishing of my wellies as they scythed their way through the long, wet grass. I was staring straight ahead at the hedge as I walked.

There it was again!

The hedge seemed to shake and then stop.

I was quite close now, but I still couldn't see anything.

I stared hard at the area of the movement, but there was nothing…all was still.

I glanced to my left to see where Gerry was. He was sitting about six feet away from me, completely upright and alert. His mouth closed, his ears pricked…he had seen the movement too and was also transfixed on the hedge.

He looked over at me and then back at the hedge again. His glance was almost human-like, as if to say, "What the heck is it?"

I started to walk nearer…I was mesmerised. I just kept staring, trying to make it out. …then as I got closer and closer, the hedge moved again…and then I saw it!

It WAS a face…

It startled me for a moment, but then thankfully, I realised what I was looking at as my eyes formed the shape of…a sheep!

It then dawned on me what was happening. It had its head stuck in the barbed wire fence that ran along the hedgerow.

"Get back, Gerry," I said as I shooed him away from his inquisitive sniffing; although the sheep was remarkably calm, considering what was happening…or it seemed that way anyhow.

I got right up close, and I could see that it was bleeding around its neck in its efforts to set itself free.

I immediately grabbed the top and bottom wire that was keeping it prisoner and pulled it apart as best I could.

The sheep struggled again for a few seconds…then thankfully, it pulled itself free!

I watched as it trotted down the bank behind the hedge…and then, it disappeared into the gloom.

Phew…! Thank goodness. That could've been a lot worse.

I turned to see where Gerry was.

He was sitting bolt upright again, about five yards away, and it looked like he had something in his mouth.

"Drop it, drop it," I said as I quickly moved towards him.

He didn't but just sat there with his head bowed; his eyes looking at me sheepishly (excuse the pun).

I put my hand to his mouth and took out what he was holding.

It was an old spoon. I could see it quite clearly in the fading light.

I was about to throw it back down on the grass, when something made me stop and take a second look.

It was a silver spoon, with a long black plastic handle.

I stared at it. Yes, it was just a spoon. It was just a spoon, with a black plastic handle BUT…as I turned it over and examined the back, it felt rough. The handle surface was rippled and course on the back.

Oh my goodness! I don't believe it!

My mind switched straight back to Mr Scary, and I immediately looked around the field in a very apprehensive manner. I started to feel very uneasy as suddenly every hedge and tree took on a different essence. I felt a shiver run down my spine as I scoured the borders of the field in the dimming light.

Oh come on, how can a farmer's field be eerie? Well, this one had suddenly taken on the role, and it was doing a good job. I felt like I was being watched from behind every bush and hedge.

This was ridiculous! Absolutely ridiculous!

I looked back down at the spoon.

It was absurd to even THINK that this could be the same one!

I stood motionless, staring at it and then glancing up and around the field again.

Gerry started to nudge my leg with his nose.

"Yep, good idea…let's get out of here."

I got back to the barn; and after first going next door to the farmer to tell him about the sheep, I relayed what had just happened to my family, and I presented them with the spoon.

"Don't be so daft!" was my wife's reaction.

"How can it POSSIBLY be the same one?"

I know, I know…and I know what you the reader are thinking too.

It CANNOT be the same spoon, but I'll tell you now…it flamin' well looks like it!

We had a few more days left at the barn; and every time I walked down into and through this particular field, I felt quite unnerved!

Even in the early blue-skied morning, with the sun beaming down, the occasional baa of a sheep and the friendly summer sounds of birds in the trees and hedgerows, I STILL felt uneasy.

The sheep's face from the other day hadn't helped. It was quite an eerie thing to see in the distance; especially as I couldn't make it out immediately…your mind just conjures up all sorts of weird images as it tries to focus on what is being presented.

I kept the spoon, and it can be found in the cutlery drawer in our house in Somerset, and I use it often. In fact, when the table is laid for dinner, it is always placed at my setting, ready for my dessert…and I play jokes on my 'children' with the spoon, occasionally throwing it onto the living-room floor whilst they are watching TV, making out that it has fallen from the skies!

It's crazy I know to even think that it could be the same one. But I somehow KNOW it is!

Goodness knows how it managed to surface again in a remote part of Devon…but it did.

I've had no dealings with Mr Scary since back then that I know of, and I certainly DO NOT want any repeat performances.

But the spoon will stay with me…

…Well, unless it disappears again…

Epilogue

Now that I am older, and perhaps just that teeny bit wiser, it does make me wonder how I mentally managed those two weeks.

I'm quite sure, that if I was experiencing all of it now, this book would have been oh so much shorter, as I certainly would not have been able to endure the mental stress of it all.

As the years go by, ones ways of thinking most definitely change, and we become less tolerant; and in my case certainly, much more cynical; and I'm sure we become less likely to take risks and chances...and I do think now in hindsight, that I probably did take quite a big risk at the time for allowing myself to be continually exposed to all of the absurdity that was going on.

Yes, I was worried and concerned, and I was scared too; but as I mentioned...I was almost 'enjoying' the experience in a weird and whacky, illogical sort of way. I am convinced though that it was my particular attitude at the time that carried me through it all. Being in my early 20s, I was very fun and party-orientated, with no real responsibilities other than work; and the explorative and adventure-seeking side of me was quite pronounced.

The serious, more-organised side of life had not kicked in yet, and I was quite happy, allowing life to organise me...and so, I just adapted myself to the situation without any consequential thoughts.

Over the years, leading up to the spoon finding, I can honestly say that the experience of the flat has never been in the forefront of my thoughts...but it has never gone away.

It's tucked away in some corner of my overactive mind (probably high up!), waiting for an opportunity to channel itself back into the limelight. And every now and then, that is exactly what it does, but really only in a story-telling way; perhaps in an effort to beat someone else's whacky yarn.

Have you ever seen the Steven Spielberg's film *Jaws,* where the three main characters are sitting in the cabin of a boat, and are trying to out-do each other with tall tales of how they received their various skin scars? Well, that's about the level of it all with me too. It's certainly not like I've been suffering from post-traumatic stress disorder or anything like that. I certainly do not go around worrying about it all, with feelings of dread and anxiety!

It was a very extraordinary happening that took place in my life, and it did affect me at the time, but it is all done and dusted as far as I'm concerned…and I do not have any constant nagging needs to do anything about it.

I've never forgotten what Johnny said though, when he intimated that Mr Scary was inside my head and was using me as a host. I have explored the suspicion that it was in fact ME somehow generating all the scary things in the flat. That it was my mind subconsciously making things move and happen, and that Mr Scary was just my explanation for it all at the time. Remember, it was only me that could feel the woolly closed-in feeling in the flat all the time.

I have given thought also to the experience of the 'non-existent' police car that was chasing me when I had returned to live with my parents. Mike said that he never saw it, which I still find unbelievable to this day! We had many discussions about it afterwards, but he swore that there was never a car. So did I therefore imagine it? I'm sure I didn't, I know I didn't! The car was real, as was the outstretched hand. And was that Mr Scary driving the car? Was it he who prevented me from going on further because he knew of the upcoming accident? Carla did once say that she felt he cared about me. I don't know, I really don't know…it's all complete speculation.

I even wondered about 'Jock' the taxi driver. Was he Mr Scary too? Did he sense my concern (and I was truly concerned) that I wasn't going to be able to get back home that night, and he somehow made Jock help me? It's all crazy stuff; it really is.

Like I said, it may have just been a particular time in my life when my mind was somehow extraordinarily active and was able to create events and react to things subconsciously without my conscious mind knowing anything about it.

Boy, I'm certainly not going to think too deeply about that idea. It's giving my conscious mind a headache now!

I can remember some friends of mine once telling me that they had a succession of weird happenings that occurred in their living room. They would come down the stairs in the morning to find furniture moved, ornaments lying on their sides, and fireplace tools would be twisted and bent.

They 'blamed' this on their young daughter for some reason; and after a short period of time, it all stopped, and it never happened again. I know it's not really comparable with the depths of my experiences, but it is comparable in that it only lasted for a short period of time.

So here we are...we're right at the end of the book...and before I finish, I would just like to mention the spoon again.

If that hadn't of come to light, I doubt whether I would have really written anything at all, as it was the spoon that made me start thinking about it all again!

And I know that it is very unrealistic and improbable of me to truly believe that it really is the same one that disappeared from my flat in 1986.

But sometimes, very unrealistic and improbable things happen, don't they...